"Would you like me for a brother-in-law, Mary Jane?"

She wouldn't like him for a brother-in-law; she would like him for a husband, and why should she suddenly discover *that*, now of all times, sitting opposite him, being cross-examined as though she were in a witness-box, and fighting a great wish to fling her arms around his neck and tell him that she loved him? It was clear Sir Thomas Latimar preferred her beautiful sister, Felicity, so he would hardly welcome Mary Jane throwing herself at him, too!

Betty Neels spent her childhood and youth in Devonshire before training as a nurse and midwife. She was an army nursing sister during the war, married a Dutchman and subsequently lived in Holland for fourteen years. She lives with her husband in Dorset, and has a daughter and grandson. Her hobbies are reading, animals, old buildings and writing. Betty started to write on retirement from nursing, incited by a lady in a library bemoaning the lack of romantic novels.

Books by Betty Neels

HARLEQUIN ROMANCE
3371—WEDDING BELLS FOR BEATRICE
3389—A CHRISTMAS WISH
3400—WAITING FOR DEBORAH
3415—THE BACHELOR'S WEDDING

Don't miss any of our special offers. Write to us at the following address for information on our newest releases.

Harlequin Reader Service
U.S.: 3010 Walden Ave., P.O. Box 1325, Buffalo, NY 14269
Canadian: P.O. Box 609, Fort Erie, Ont. L2A 5X3

Dearest
Mary Jane
Betty Neels

Harlequin Books

TORONTO • NEW YORK • LONDON
AMSTERDAM • PARIS • SYDNEY • HAMBURG
STOCKHOLM • ATHENS • TOKYO • MILAN
MADRID • WARSAW • BUDAPEST • AUCKLAND

ISBN 0-373-03435-0

DEAREST MARY JANE

First North American Publication 1996.

CHAPTER ONE

IT WAS five o'clock and the warm hazy sunshine of a September afternoon was dwindling into the evening's coolness. The Misses Potter, sitting at a table in the window of the tea-shop, put down their teacups reluctantly and prepared to leave. Miss Emily, the elder of the two ladies, rammed her sensible hat more firmly on her head and addressed the girl sitting behind the tiny counter at the back of the room.

'If we might have our bill, Mary Jane?'

The girl came to the table and the two ladies looked at her, wondering, as they frequently did, how whoever had chosen the girl's name could have guessed how aptly it fitted. She looked like a Mary Jane, not tall, a little too thin, with an unremarkable face and light brown hair, straight and long and pinned in an untidy swirl on top of her head. Only when she looked at you the violet eyes, fringed with long curling lashes, made one forget her prosaic person.

She said now in her quiet voice, 'I hope you enjoyed your tea. In another week or two I'll start making teacakes.'

Her customers nodded in unison. 'We shall look forward to that.' Miss Emily opened her purse. 'We mustn't keep you, it's closing time.' She put money on the table and Mary Jane opened the door and waited until they were across the village street before closing it.

She cleared the table, carried everything into the small kitchen behind the tea-room and went to turn the notice to 'Closed' on the door just as a car drew up outside. The door was thrust open before she had time to turn the key and a man came in. He was massively built and tall, so that the small room became even smaller.

'Good,' he said briskly. 'You're not closed. My companion would like tea . . .'

'But I am closed,' said Mary Jane in a reasonable voice. 'I'm just locking the door, only you pushed it open. You are not very far from Stow-on-the-Wold—there are several hotels there, you'll get tea quite easily.'

The man spoke evenly, rather as though he were addressing a child or someone hard of hearing. 'My companion doesn't wish to wait any longer. A pot of tea is all I am asking for; surely that isn't too much?'

He sounded like a man who liked his own way and got it, but Mary Jane had a lot to do before she could go to her bed; besides, she disliked being browbeaten. 'I'm sorry . . .'

She was interrupted by the girl who swept into the tea-room. No, not a girl, decided Mary Jane, a woman in her thirties and beautiful, although her looks were marred by her frown and tight mouth.

'Where's my tea?' she demanded. 'Good lord, Thomas, all I want is a cup of tea. Is that too much to ask for? What is this dump, anyway?' She flung herself gracefully into one of the little cane chairs. 'I suppose it will be undrinkable tea-bags, but if there's nothing else . . .'

Mary Jane gave the man an icy violet stare. 'I do have drinkable tea-bags,' she told him, 'but perhaps the lady would prefer Earl Grey or Orange Pekoe?'

'Earl Grey,' snapped the woman, 'and I hope I shan't have to wait too long.'

'Just while the kettle boils,' said Mary Jane in a dangerously gentle voice.

She went into the kitchen and laid a tray and made the tea and carried it to the table and was very surprised when the man got up and took the tray from her.

In the kitchen she started clearing up. There would be a batch of scones to make after she had had her supper and the sugar bowls to fill and the jam dishes to see to as well as the pastry to make ready for the sausage rolls she served during the lunch-hour. She was putting the last of the crockery away when the man came to the doorway. 'The bill?' he asked.

She went behind the counter and made it out and handed it silently to him and the woman called across. 'I imagine there is no ladies' room here?'

Mary Jane paused in counting change. 'No.' She added deliberately, 'The public lavatories are on the other side of the village square on the road to Moreton.'

The man bit off a laugh and then said with cool politeness, 'Thank you for giving us tea.' He ushered his companion out of the door, turning as he did so to turn the notice to 'Closed'.

Mary Jane watched him drive away. It was a nice car—a dark blue Rolls-Royce. There was a lonely stretch of road before they reached Stow-on-the-Wold, and she hoped they would run out of petrol. It was unlikely, though, he didn't strike her as that kind of man.

She locked the door, tidied the small room with its four tables and went through to the kitchen where she washed the last of the tea things, put her supper in the oven and went up the narrow staircase tucked away behind a door by the dresser. Upstairs, she went first to her bedroom, a low-ceilinged room with a latticed window overlooking the back garden and furnished rather sparsely. The curtains were pretty, however, as was the bedspread and there were flowers in a bowl on the old-fashioned dressing-table. She tidied herself without wasting too much time about it, and crossed the tiny landing to the living-room at the front of the cottage. Quite a large room since it was over the tea-room, and furnished as sparsely as the bedroom. There were flowers here too, and a small gas fire in the tiled grate which she lighted before switching on a reading lamp by the small armchair, so that the room looked welcoming. That done, she went downstairs again to open the kitchen door to allow Brimble, her cat, to come in—a handsome tabby who, despite his cat-flap, preferred to come in and out like anyone else. He wreathed himself round her legs now, wanting his supper and, when she had fed him, went upstairs to lie before the gas fire.

Mary Jane took the shepherd's pie out of the oven, laid the table under the kitchen window and sat down to eat her supper, listening with half an ear to the last of the six o'clock news while she planned her baking for the next day. The bus went into Stow-on-the-Wold on Fridays, returning around four o'clock, and those passengers who lived on the outskirts of the village frequently came in for a pot of tea before they set off for home.

She finished the pie and ate an apple, cleared the table and got out her pastry board and rolling pin. Scones were easy to make and were always popular. She did two batches and then saw to the sausage rolls before going into the tea-room to count the day's takings. Hardly a fortune; she just about paid her way but there was nothing over for holidays or new clothes, though the cottage was hers...

Uncle Matthew had left it to her when he had died two years previously. He had been her guardian ever since her own parents had been killed in their car. She and Felicity, who was older than she was, had been schoolgirls and their uncle and aunt had given them a home and educated them. Felicity, with more than her fair share of good looks, had taken herself off to London as soon as she had left school and had become a successful model, while Mary Jane had stayed at home to run the house for an ailing aunt and an uncle who, although kind, didn't bother with her overmuch. When her aunt had died she had stayed on, looking after him and the house, trying not to think about the future and the years flying by. She had been almost twenty-three when her uncle died and, to her astonished delight, left her the cottage he had owned in the village and five hundred pounds. She had moved into it from his large house at the other end of the village as soon as she could, for Uncle Matthew's heir had disliked her on sight and so had his wife...

She had spent some of the money on second-hand furniture and then, since she had no skills other than that of a good cook, she had opened the tea-room. She was known and liked in the village, which was a help, and after a few uncertain months she was making just enough to live on and pay the bills. Felicity had been to see her, amused at the whole set-up but offering no help. 'You always were the domestic type,' she had observed laughingly. 'I'd die if I had to spend my days here, you know. I'm going to the Caribbean to do some modelling next week—don't you wish you were me?'

Mary Jane had considered the question. 'No, not really,' she said finally. 'I do hope you have a lovely time.'

'I intend to, though the moment I set eyes on a handsome rich man I shall marry him.' She gave Mary Jane a friendly pat on the shoulder. 'Not much hope of that happening to you, darling.'

Mary Jane had agreed pleasantly, reflecting that just to set eyes on a man who hadn't lived all his life in the village and was either married or about to be married would be nice.

She remembered that now as she took the last lot of sausage rolls out of the oven. She had certainly met a man that very afternoon and, unless he had borrowed that car, he was at least comfortably off and handsome to boot. A pity that they hadn't fallen in love with each other at first sight, the way characters did in books. Rather the reverse: he had shown no desire to meet her again and she hadn't liked him. She cleared up once more and went upstairs to sit with Brimble by the fire and presently she went to bed.

It was exactly a week later when Miss Emily Potter came into the shop at the unusual hour—for her—of eleven o'clock in the morning.

Beyond an elderly couple and a young man on a motorbike in a great hurry, Mary Jane had had no customers, which was a good thing, for Miss Emily was extremely agitated.

'I did not know which way to turn,' she began breathlessly, 'and then I thought of you, Mary Jane. Mrs Stokes is away, you know, and Miss Kemble over at the rectory has the young mothers' and toddlers' coffee-morning. The taxi is due in a short time and dear Mabel is quite overwrought.'

Mary Jane saw that she would have to get to the heart of the matter quickly before Miss Emily became distraught as well. 'Why?'

Miss Potter gave her a startled look. 'She has to see this specialist—her hip, you know. Dr Fellows made the appointment but now she is most unwilling to go. So unfortunate, for this specialist comes very rarely to Cheltenham and the appointment is for two o'clock and I cannot possibly go with her, Didums is poorly and cannot be left...'

'You would like me to have Didums?' asked Mary Jane and sighed inwardly. Didums was a particularly awkward pug dog with a will of her own; Brimble wouldn't like her at all.

'No, no—dear Didums would never go with anyone but myself or my sister. If you would go with Mabel?' Miss Potter gazed rather wildly around the tea-room. 'There's no one here; you could close for an hour or two.'

Mary Jane forbore from pointing out that although there was no one there at the moment, any minute now the place might be filled with people demanding coffee and biscuits. It wasn't likely but there was always a chance. 'When would we get back?' she asked cautiously.

'Well, if the appointment is for two o'clock I don't suppose she will be very long, do you? I'm sure you should be back by four o'clock...'

Miss Potter wrung her hands. 'Oh, dear, I have no idea what to do.'

The taxi would take something over half an hour to get to the hospital. Mary Jane supposed that they would need to get there with half an hour to spare.

'I believe that there is a very good place in the hospital where you can get coffee—dear Mabel will need refreshment.'

Mary Jane thought that after a ride in the taxi with the overwrought Miss Mabel Potter she might be in need of refreshment herself. She said in her calm way, 'I'll be over in half an hour or so, Miss Potter. There's still plenty of time.'

A tearfully grateful Miss Potter went on her way. Mary Jane closed the tea-room, changed into a blouse and skirt and a cardigan, drank a cup of coffee and ate a scone, made sure that Brimble was cosily asleep on the end of her bed and walked across the village square and along the narrow country lane which led to the Misses Potter's cottage. It was called a cottage but, in fact, it was a rather nice house built of Cotswold stone and much too large for them. They had been born there and intended to live out their lives there, even though they were forced to do so as economically as possible. Mary Jane went up the garden path, rang the bell and was admitted by Miss Emily and led to the drawing-room where Miss Mabel sat surrounded by furniture which had been there before she was born and which neither she nor her sister would dream of changing.

Mary Jane sat down on a nice little Victorian button-back chair and embarked on a cheerful conversation. It was rather like talking to someone condemned to the guillotine; Miss Mabel bore the appearance of someone whose last moment had come. It was a relief when the taxi arrived and the cheerful conversation was scrapped for urgent persuasions to get in.

They were half an hour too early for their appointment, which was a mistake, for the orthopaedic clinic, although it had started punctually, was already running late. It was going on for three o'clock by the time the severe-looking sister called Miss Potter's name and by then she was in such a nervous state that Mary Jane had a job getting her on to her feet and into the consulting-room.

The consultant sitting behind the desk got up and shook Miss Potter's nerveless hand—the man who had demanded tea for his tiresome companion. Mary Jane, never one to think before she spoke, said chattily, 'Oh, hello—it's you—fancy seeing you here.'

She received a look from icy blue eyes in which there was no hint of recollection, although his 'Good afternoon' was uttered with detached civility and she blushed, something she did far too easily however much she tried not to. The stern-faced sister took no notice. She said briskly, 'You had better stay with Miss Potter, she seems nervous.'

Mary Jane sat herself down in a corner of the room where Miss Potter could see her and watched the man wheedle that lady's complaints and symptoms out of her. He did it very kindly and without any sign of impatience, even when Miss Potter sidetracked to explain about the marmalade which hadn't jelled be-

cause she had felt poorly and hadn't given it her full
attention. A nasty, arrogant man, Mary Jane decided, but he had his good points. She had thought
about him once or twice of course, and with a touch
of wistfulness, for handsome giants who drove Rolls-
Royce motor cars weren't exactly thick on the ground
in her part of the world, but she hadn't expected to
see him again. She wondered about his beautiful
companion and was roused from her thoughts by
Sister leading Miss Mabel away to a curtained-off
corner to be examined.

The man took no notice of Mary Jane but wrote
steadily and very fast until Sister came to tell him that
his patient was ready.

He disappeared behind the curtain and Mary Jane,
bored with sitting still and sure that he would be at
least ten minutes, got up and went over to the desk
and peered down at the notes he had been writing.
She wasn't surprised that she could hardly make head
or tail of it, for he had been writing fast, but presently
she began to make sense of it. There were some rough
diagrams too, with arrows pointing in all directions
and what looked like Latin. It was a pity that no one
had seen to it that he wrote a legible hand when he
was a schoolboy.

His voice, gently enquiring as to whether she was
interested in orthopaedics, sent her whirling round to
bump into his waistcoat.

'Yes—no, that is...' She had gone scarlet again.
'Your writing is quite unreadable,' she finished.

'Yes? But as long as I can read it...you're a nosy
young woman.'

'The patients' charter,' said Mary Jane, never at a
loss for a word. He gave rather a nasty laugh.

'And a busybody as well,' he observed.

He sat down at his desk again and started to write once more and she went back to her chair and watched him. About thirty-five, she supposed, with brown hair already grizzled at the sides, and the kind of commanding nose he could look down. A firm mouth and a strong chin. She supposed that he could be quite nice when he smiled. He was dressed with understated elegance, the kind which cost a great deal of money, and she wondered what his name was. Not that it mattered, she reminded herself, as Miss Mabel came from behind the curtain, fully dressed even to her hat and gloves.

He got up as she came towards him and Mary Jane liked him for that, and for the manner in which he broke the news to his patient that an operation on her hip would relieve her of pain and disability.

He turned to Mary Jane. 'You are a relation of Miss Potter?' His tone was politely impersonal.

'Me? No. Just someone in the village. Miss Potter's sister couldn't come because of Didums...' His raised eyebrows forced her to explain. 'Their dog—she's not very well, the vet said...' She stopped. It was obvious that he didn't want to know what the vet had said.

'Perhaps you could ask Miss Potter's sister to ring the hospital and she will be told what arrangements will be made to admit her sister.'

He addressed himself to Miss Mabel once more, got to his feet to bid her goodbye, nodded at Mary Jane and Sister ushered them out into the waiting-room again.

'What is his name?' asked Mary Jane.

Sister had her hand on the next case sheets. She gave Mary Jane a frosty look. 'If you mean the consultant you have just seen, his name is Sir Thomas Latimer. Miss Potter is extremely lucky that he will take her as a patient.' She added impressively, 'He is famous in his field.'

'Oh, good.' Mary Jane gave Sister a sunny smile and guided Miss Mabel out of the hospital and into the forecourt where the taxi was parked.

The return journey was entirely taken up with Miss Mabel's rather muddled version of her examination, the driver's rather lurid account of his wife's varicose veins and their treatment and Mary Jane doing her best to guide the conversation into neutral topics.

It took some time to explain everything once they had reached the cottage. Mary Jane's sensible account interlarded with Miss Mabel's flights of fancy, but presently she was able to wish them goodbye and go home. Brimble was waiting for her, wanting his tea and company. She fed him, made a pot of tea for herself and, since it was almost five o'clock by now, she made no attempt to open the tea-room. She locked up and went upstairs and sat down by the gas fire with Brimble on her lap, thinking of Sir Thomas Latimer.

Nothing happened for several days; the fine weather held and Mary Jane reaped a better harvest than usual from motorists making the best of the last of summer. She had seen nothing of the Misses Potter but she hadn't expected to; they came once a week, as regular as clockwork, on a Thursday to draw their pensions and indulge themselves with tea and scones, so she looked up in surprise when they came into the tea-room at eleven o'clock in the morning, two days early.

'We have had a letter,' observed Miss Emily, 'which we should like you to read, Mary Jane, since it concerns you. And since we are here, I think that we might indulge ourselves with a cup of your excellent coffee.'

Mary Jane poured the coffee and took the letter she was offered. It was very clearly worded: Miss Mabel was to present herself at the hospital in four days' time so that the operation found necessary by Sir Thomas Latimer might be carried out. Mary Jane skimmed over the bit about bringing a nightgown and toiletries and slowed at the next paragraph. It was considered advisable, in view of Miss Mabel's nervous disposition, that the young lady who had accompanied her on her previous visit should do so again so that Miss Potter might be reassured by her company.

'Well, I never,' said Mary Jane and gave the letter back.

'You will do this?' asked Miss Emily in a voice which expected Mary Jane to say yes. 'Most fortunately, you have few customers at this time of year, and an hour or so away will do you no great harm.'

Mary Jane forbore from pointing out that with the fine weather she could reasonably expect enough coffee and tea drinkers, not to mention scone eaters, to make it well worth her while to stay open from nine o'clock until five o'clock. The good weather wouldn't last and business was slack during the winter months. However, she liked the Misses Potter.

'Three o'clock,' she said. 'That means leaving here some time after two o'clock, doesn't it? Yes, of course I'll go and see Miss Mabel safely settled in.'

The ladies looked so relieved that she refilled their cups and didn't charge them for it. 'I hope,' commented Miss Emily, 'that Didums will be well

enough for me to leave her so that I may visit Mabel.
I do not know how long she will be in the hospital.'

'I'll try and find out for you.' The tea-room door
opened and four people came in and she left them to
their coffee while she attended to her new customers:
two elderly couples who ate a gratifying number of
scones and ordered a pot of coffee. Mary Jane took
it as a sign that obliging the Misses Potter when she
really hadn't wanted to would be rewarded by more
customers than usual and more money in the till.

Indeed, it seemed that that was the case; she was
kept nicely busy for the next few days so that she
turned the 'Open' notice to 'Closed' with reluctance.
It was another lovely day, and more people than usual
had come in for coffee and if today was anything like
yesterday she could have filled the little tea-room for
most of the afternoon...

Miss Mabel wore an air of stunned resignation,
getting into the taxi without needing to be coaxed,
and Mary Jane's warm heart was wrung by the un-
happiness on her companion's face. She strove to find
cheerful topics of conversation, chattering away in a
manner most unusual for her so that by the time they
reached the hospital her tongue was cleaving to the
roof of her mouth. At least there was no delay; they
were taken at once to the ward and Miss Potter was
invited to undress and get into bed while Mary Jane
recited necessary information to the ward clerk, a jolly,
friendly woman who gave her a leaflet about visiting
and telephoning and information as to where the
canteen was. 'Sister will be coming along in a minute;
you might like a word with her.'

Mary Jane went back to Miss Potter's cubicle and found that lady was lying in bed, looking pale although she mustered a smile.

'Sister's coming to see you in a minute,' said Mary Jane. 'I'll take your clothes back with me, shall I, and bring them again when you're getting up?' She cocked an ear at the sound of feet coming down the ward. 'Here's Sister.'

It was Sir Thomas Latimer as well, in a long white coat, his hands in his trouser pockets. He wished Miss Potter a cheerful good afternoon, gave Mary Jane a cool stare and addressed himself to his patient.

He had a lovely bedside manner, Mary Jane reflected, soothing and friendly and yet conveying the firm impression that whatever he said or did would be right. Mary Jane watched Miss Potter relax, even smile a little, and edged towards the curtains; if he was going to examine his patient he wouldn't want her there.

'Stay,' he told her without turning his head.

She very much wanted to say 'I shan't,' but Miss Potter's precarious calm must not be disturbed. She gave the back of his head a look to pierce his skull and stayed where she was.

She had had a busy day and she was a little tired. She eased herself from one foot to the other and wished she could be like Sister, standing on the other side of the bed. A handsome woman, still young and obviously highly efficient. She and Sir Thomas exchanged brief remarks from time to time, none of which made sense to her, not that they were meant to. She stifled a yawn, smiled at Miss Potter and eased a foot out of a shoe.

Sister might be efficient, she was kind too; Miss
Potter was getting more and more cheerful by the
minute, and when Sir Thomas finally finished and sat
down on her side of the bed she smiled, properly this
time, and took the hand he offered her, listening to
his reassuring voice. It was when he said, 'Now I think
we might let Miss…?' that he turned to look at Mary
Jane.

'Seymour,' she told him frostily, cramming her foot
back into its shoe.

His eyes went from her face to her feet, his face
expressionless.

'Miss Potter may be visited the day after tomorrow.
Her sister is free to telephone whenever she wishes to.
I shall operate tomorrow morning at eight o'clock.
Miss Potter should be back in her bed well before
noon.' He added, 'You are on the telephone?'

'Me? No. We use the post office and Miss Kemble
at the rectory will take a message. Everyone knows
the Misses Potter. I've given the ward clerk several
numbers she can ring. But someone will phone at noon
tomorrow.'

He nodded, smiled very kindly at his patient and
went away with Sister as a young nurse took their
place. The promise of a cup of tea made Mary Jane's
departure easier. She kissed the elderly cheek. 'We'll
all be in to see you,' she promised, and took herself
off to find the taxi and its patient driver.

By the time they were back in the village and she
had explained everything to Miss Emily it was far too
late to open the tea-room. She made herself a pot of
tea, fed Brimble, and padded around in her stockinged
feet getting everything ready for the batch of scones

she still had to make ready for the next day. While
she did it she thought about Sir Thomas.

The operation was a success; the entire village knew
about it and, since they foregathered in Mary Jane's
tea-room to discuss it, she was kept busy with pots of
tea and coffee. Miss Kemble, being the rector's sister,
offered to drive to the hospital on the following day.
'The car will take four—you will come of course, Miss
Emily, and Mrs Stokes, how fortunate that she is
back—and of course my brother.'

Miss Emily put down her cup. 'It would be nice if
Mary Jane could come too....'

'Another day,' said Miss Kemble bossily. 'Besides,
who is to look after Didums? You know she is good
with Mary Jane.'

So it was agreed and the next day, encouraged by
Sister's report that Miss Mabel had had a good night,
they set off. Mary Jane watched them go holding a
peevish Didums under one arm. She took the dog up
to the sitting-room presently and closed the door,
thankful that Brimble was taking a nap on her bed
and hadn't noticed anything. She would have liked to
have visited Miss Mabel and now she would have to
wait until she could find someone who would give her
a lift into Cheltenham.

As it turned out, she didn't have to wait long; Mrs
Fellowes popped in for a cup of tea and wanted to
know why Mary Jane hadn't gone with the others.
'That's too bad,' she declared, 'but not to worry. I'm
driving the doctor to Cheltenham on Sunday—about
three o'clock, we'll give you a lift in, only we shan't
be coming back. Do you suppose you can get back
here? There's a bus leaves Cheltenham for Stratford-
upon-Avon, so you could get to Broadway...' She

frowned. 'It's a long way round, but I'm sure there's an evening bus to Stow-on-the-Wold from there.'

Mary Jane said recklessly, 'Thank you very much, I'd like a lift. I'm sure I can get a bus home. I'll have a look at the timetable in the post office.'

It was going to be an awkward, roundabout journey home and it would depend on her getting on to the bus in Cheltenham. She would have to keep a sharp eye on the time; the bus depot was some way from the hospital. All the same she would go. She wrote a postcard telling Miss Mabel that she would see her on Sunday afternoon and put it in the letterbox before she could have second, more prudent thoughts.

Miss Emily, coming to collect Didums, had a great deal to say. Her sister was doing well, Sister had said, and she was to get out of bed on the following day. 'Modern surgery,' observed Miss Potter with a shake of the head. 'In my youth we stayed in bed for weeks. That nice man—he operated; Sir someone—came to see her while I was there and told me that the operation had been most successful and that dear Mabel would greatly benefit from it. Nice manners, too.'

Mary Jane muttered under her breath and offered Miss Potter a cup of tea.

She was quite busy for the rest of that week, so that she felt justified on Sunday in taking enough money from the till to cover her journey back home. If the worst came to the worst she could have a taxi; it would mean going without new winter boots, but she liked Miss Mabel.

She usually stayed open for part of Sunday, for that was when motorists tended to stop for tea, but she locked up after lunch, made sure that Brimble was safely indoors and walked through the village to the doctor's house.

Miss Mabel was delighted to see her; she seemed to have taken on a new lease of life since her operation and she insisted on telling Mary Jane every single detail of the treatment. She had got to the momentous moment when she had been out of bed when there was a slight stir in the ward. Sir Thomas Latimer was coming towards them, indeed, he appeared to be about to pass them when he stopped at Miss Mabel's bed.

On his bi-weekly round he had seen Mary Jane's postcard on Miss Mabel's locker and, without quite knowing why, he had decided to be on the ward on Sunday afternoon. It had been easy enough to give a reason—he had operated the day before on an emergency case and what could be more normal than a visit from him to see how his patient progressed? His casual, 'Good afternoon,' was a masterpiece of surprise.

Mary Jane's polite response was quite drowned by Miss Mabel's voice. 'Is it not delightful?' she enquired of him. 'Mary Jane has come to visit me—Dr Fellowes gave her a lift here. She will have to return by bus, though. I'm not sure how she will manage that, it being a Sunday, but she tells me that she has everything arranged.' She beamed at Mary Jane, who wasn't looking. 'I have been telling her how excellent is the treatment here. I shall recommend it to my friends.'

Just as though it were an hotel, thought Mary Jane, carefully not looking at Sir Thomas.

He stayed only a few minutes, bidding them both goodbye with casual politeness, and Mary Jane settled down to hear the rest of Miss Mabel's experiences, until a glance at the clock told her that she would have to go at once if she were to catch the bus. Not easily done, however, for Miss Mabel suddenly thought of numerous messages for her sister so that Mary Jane fairly galloped out of the hospital to pause at the entrance to get her bearings. She wasn't quite sure where the bus depot was and Mrs Fellowes' kindly directions had been vague.

The Rolls-Royce whispered to a halt beside her and its door opened.

'Get in,' said Sir Thomas. 'I'm going through your village.'

'I'm catching a bus.'

'Very unlikely. The Sunday service leaves half an hour earlier—I have that from the head porter, who is never wrong about anything.' He added gently, 'Get in, Miss Seymour, before we are had up for loitering.'

'But I'm not...' she began, and caught his eye. 'All right.' She sounded ungracious. 'Thank you.'

She fastened the seatbelt and sat back in luxury and he drove off without saying anything. Indeed, he didn't speak at all for some time, and then only to observe that Miss Mabel would be returning home very shortly. Mary Jane replied suitably and lapsed into silence once more for the simple reason that she had no idea what to talk about, but as they neared the village she made an effort. 'Do you live near here?'

'No, in London. I have to live near my work.'

'Then why are you here?'

'I visit various hospitals whenever it is found necessary.'

A most unsatisfactory answer. She didn't say anything more until he drew up before the tea-room.

He got out before she could open her door and opened it for her, took the old-fashioned key from her and opened the cottage door.

It was dusk now and he found the switch and turned on the lights before standing aside to let her pass him.

'Thank you very much,' said Mary Jane once again, and bent to pick up Brimble who had rushed to meet her.

Sir Thomas leaned against the half-open door in no hurry to go. 'Your cat?'

'Yes, Brimble. He's—he's company.'

'You live alone?'

'Yes.' She peered up at him. 'You'd better go, Sir Thomas, if you're going all the way to London.'

Sir Thomas agreed meekly. He had never, he reflected, been told to go by a girl. On the contrary, they made a point of asking him to stay. He wasn't a conceited man but now he was intrigued. He had wanted to meet her again, going deliberately to the hospital when he knew that she would be there, wanting to know more about her. The drive had hardly been successful. He bade her a pleasantly impersonal goodbye. They were unlikely to meet again. He dismissed her from his thoughts and drove back to London.

CHAPTER TWO

SEPTEMBER was almost over and the weather was changing. Fewer and fewer tourists stopped for coffee or tea although Mary Jane still did a steady trade with the village dwellers—just enough to keep the bills paid. Miss Mabel made steady progress and Mary Jane, graciously offered a lift in the rectory car, visited her again. Sir Thomas had been again, she was told, and Miss Mabel was to return home in a week's time and see him when he came to the hospital in six weeks' time. 'Such a nice man,' sighed Miss Mabel, 'a true gentleman, if you know what I mean.'

Mary Jane wasn't too sure about that but she murmured obligingly.

Miss Mabel's homecoming was something of an event in a village where one day was very like another. The ambulance brought her, deposited her gently in her home, drained Mary Jane's teapots and ate almost all the scones, and departed to be replaced by Miss Kemble, Mrs Stokes and after an interval Dr Fellowes, who tactfully sent them all away and made sure that the Misses Potter were allowed peace and quiet. Mary Jane, slipping through the village with a plate of tea-cakes as a welcome home gift, was prevailed upon to stay for a few minutes while Miss Mabel reiterated her experiences. 'I am to walk each day,' she said proudly, 'but lead a quiet life.' She laughed and Miss Emily laughed too. 'Not that we do anything else, do we, Mary Jane?'

Mary Jane smilingly agreed; that she had dreams of lovely clothes, candlelit dinners for two, dancing night after night and always with someone who adored her, was something she kept strictly to herself. Even Felicity, on the rare occasions when she saw her, took it for granted that she was content.

The mornings were frosty now and the evenings drawing in. The village, after the excitement of Miss Mabel's operation, did settle down. Mary Jane baked fewer scones and some days customers were so few it was hardly worth keeping the tea-room open.

She was preparing to close after an unprofitable Monday when the door was thrust open and a man came in. Mary Jane, wiping down the already clean tables, looked up hopefully, saw who it was and said in a neutral voice, 'Good evening, Oliver.'

Her cousin, Uncle Matthew's heir.

She had known him since her schooldays and had disliked him from the start, just as he had disliked her. She had been given short shrift when her uncle had died and for her part she hadn't been able to leave fast enough, for not only did Oliver dislike her, his wife, a cold woman, pushing her way up the social ladder, disliked her too. She stood, the cloth in her hand, waiting for him to speak.

'Business pretty bad?' he asked.

'It's a quiet time of the year. I'm making a living, thank you, Oliver.'

She was surprised to see that he was trying to be friendly, but not for long.

'Hope you'll do something for me,' he went on. 'Margaret has to go to London to see some specialist or other about her back. I have to go to America on business and someone will have to drive her up and

stay with her.' He didn't quite meet her eyes. 'I wondered if you'd do that?' He laughed. 'Blood's thicker
than water and all that...'

'I hadn't noticed,' said Mary Jane coldly. 'Margaret
has family of her own, hasn't she? Surely there is
someone with nothing better to do who could go with
her?'

'We did ask around,' said Oliver airily, 'but you
know how it is, they lead busy social lives, they simply
can't spare the time.'

'And I can?' asked Mary Jane crisply.

'Well, you can't be making a fortune at this time
of year. It won't cost you a penny. Margaret will have
to stay the night in town—tests and so forth. She can't
drive herself because of this wretched back, and besides she's very nervous.' He added, 'She is in pain,
too.'

Mary Jane had a tender heart. Very much against
her inclination she agreed, reluctantly, to go with
Margaret. It would mean leaving Brimble alone for
two days but Mrs Adams next door would feed him
and make sure that he was safe. It would mean
shutting the tea-room too and, although Oliver made
light of the paucity of customers at that time of year,
all the same she would be short of two days' takings,
however sparse they might be.

Oliver, having got what he wanted, lost no time in
going. 'Next Tuesday,' he told her. 'I'll drive Margaret
here in the car and you can take over. I leave in the
afternoon.'

If he felt gratitude, he didn't show it. Mary Jane
watched him get into his car and pulled a face at his
back as he drove away.

Oliver returned on the Tuesday morning and Mary
Jane, having packed an overnight bag, got into her
elderly tweed suit, consigned Brimble to Mrs Adams's
kindly hands, and opened the door to him.

He didn't bother with a good morning, a nod
seemed the best he could manage. 'Margaret's in the
car. Drive carefully; you'll have to fill up with petrol,
there's not enough to bring you back.'

Mary Jane gave him a limpid look. 'Margaret has
the money for that? I haven't.'

'Good God, girl, surely a small matter of a few
gallons of petrol...'

'Well, just as you like. I'm sure Jim at the garage
will have a man who can drive Margaret—you pay by
the mile I believe, and petrol extra.'

Oliver went a dangerous plum colour. 'No one
would think that we were cousins...'

'Well, no, I don't think that they would, I quite
often forget that too.' She smiled. 'If you go now
you'll catch Jim—he'll be open by now.'

Oliver gave her a look to kill, with no effect whatsoever, and took out his wallet.

'I shall require a strict account of what you spend,'
he told her crossly, and handed her some notes. 'Now
come along, Margaret is nervous enough already.'

Margaret was tall and what she described to herself
as elegantly thin. She had good features, marred by
a down-turned mouth and a frown; moreover she had
a complaining voice. She moaned now, 'Oh, dear,
whatever has kept you? Can't you see how ill I am?
All this waiting about...'

Mary Jane got into the car. She said, 'Good
morning, Margaret.' She turned to look at her. 'Before

we go I must make it quite clear to you that I have no money with me—perhaps Oliver told you already?'

Margaret looked faintly surprised. 'No, he didn't, he said . . . well, I've enough with me for both of us.' She added sourly, 'It will be a nice treat for you, a couple of days in town, all expenses paid.'

Mary Jane let this pass and, since Oliver did no more than raise a careless hand to his wife, drove away. Margaret was going to sulk, which left Mary Jane free to indulge her thoughts. She toyed with the idea of sending Oliver a bill for two days' average takings at the tea-rooms, plus the hourly wages she would earn as a waitress. He would probably choke himself to death on reading it but it was fun to think about.

'You're driving too fast,' complained Margaret.

Oliver had booked them in at a quiet hotel, near enough to Wigmore Street for them to be able to walk there for Margaret's appointment. He had thought of everything, thought Mary Jane, unpacking Margaret's bag for her since that lady declared herself to be exhausted; a hotel so quiet and respectable that there was nothing to do and no one under fifty staying there. Her room was on the floor above Margaret's, overlooking a blank wall, furnished with what she called Hotel Furniture. She unpacked her own bag and went back to escort Margaret to lunch.

The dining-room was solid Victorian, dimly lit, the tables laden with silverware and any number of wine glasses. She cheered up at the sight; breakfast had been a sketchy affair and she was hungry and the elaborate table settings augered well for a good meal.

Unfortunately, this didn't turn out to be the case; lunch was elaborately presented but not very filling:

something fishy on a lettuce leaf, lamb chops with a small side-dish of vegetables and one potato, and trifle to follow. They drank water and Mary Jane defiantly ate two rolls.

'I cannot think,' grumbled Margaret picking at her chop, 'why Oliver booked us in at this place. When we come to town—the theatre, you know, or shopping—we always go to one of the best hotels.' She thought for a moment. 'Of course, I suppose he thought that, as you were coming with me, this would do.'

Mary Jane's eyes glowed with purple fire. 'Now, that was thoughtful of him. But you have no need to stay here, Margaret, you can get a room in any hotel, pay the bill here and I'll drive myself back this afternoon and get someone from Jim's garage to collect you tomorrow.'

'You wouldn't—how dare you suggest it? Oliver would never forgive you.'

'I don't suppose he would. I don't suppose he'd forgive you either for spending his money. I dare say it won't be so bad; you'll be home again tomorrow.'

'Oliver won't be back for at least a week.' Margaret paused. 'Why don't you come and stay with me until he is back? I shall need looking after— all the worry of this examination is really too much for me. I'm alone.'

'There's a housekeeper, isn't there? And two daily maids and the gardener?' She glanced at her watch. 'Since we have to walk to this place we had better go and get ready.'

'I feel quite ill at the very thought of being examined,' observed Margaret as they set out. She had felt well enough to make up her face very nicely and put on a fetching hat. She pushed past Mary Jane in a cloud of L'Air du Temps and told her sharply to hurry up.

Wigmore Street was quiet and dignified in the early afternoon sun and the specialist's rooms, according to the brass plate on the door, were in a tall red-brick house in the middle of a terrace of similar houses. Mary Jane rang the bell and they were ushered into a narrow hall.

'First floor,' the porter told them and went back to his cubbyhole, advising them that there was a lift if they preferred.

It was very quiet on the first-floor landing, doors on either side and one at the end. 'Ring the bell,' said Margaret and pointed to the door on the left.

It was as Mary Jane put her finger on it that she realised something. The little plate above it was inscribed Sir Thomas Latimer! She had seen it on the doorplate downstairs as well but it hadn't registered. She felt a little thrill of excitement at seeing him again. Not that she liked him in the least, she told herself, as the door was opened and Margaret swept past her, announcing her arrival in a condescending way which Mary Jane could see didn't go down well with the nurse.

They were a little early. The nurse offered chairs, made polite conversation for a few moments and went across to speak to the receptionist sitting at a desk in the corner of the room.

'I didn't expect to wait,' complained Margaret, 'I've come a long way and I'm in a good deal of pain.'

The nurse came back. 'Sir Thomas has many patients, Mrs Seymour, and some need more time than others.'

Five minutes later the door opened and an elderly lady, walking with sticks, came out accompanied by Sir Thomas, who shook her hand and handed her over to the nurse.

He went back into his consulting-room and closed the door and Mary Jane decided that he hadn't noticed her.

However, he had. He put the folder on his desk and went over to the window and looked out, surprised at the pleasure he had felt at the sight of her. He went back to his desk and opened the folder; this Mrs Seymour he was to see must be a sister-in-law—she and Mary Jane came from the same village.

He went and sat down and asked his nurse over the intercom to send in Mrs Seymour.

He could find nothing wrong with her at all; she described endless symptoms in a rather whining voice, none of which he could substantiate. Nevertheless, he sent her to the X-ray unit on the floor above and listened patiently to her renewed complaints when she returned.

'If you will return in the morning,' he told her, 'when the X-ray results will be ready, I hope that I will be able to reassure you. I can find nothing wrong with you, Mrs Seymour, but we can discuss that tomorrow. Shall we say ten o'clock?'

'He is no good,' declared Margaret as they walked back. 'I shall find another specialist . . .'

'You could at least wait and see what the X-rays show,' suggested Mary Jane sensibly. 'Why not have a rest in your room and an early night after dinner?'

First, though, they had tea in the hotel lounge and since it was, rather surprisingly, quite a substantial one, Mary Jane made the most of it, a little surprised at Margaret, despite her pain, eating a great many sandwiches and cream cakes. Left on her own, she poured a last cup of tea and thought about Sir Thomas. She hadn't expected him to recognise her and after all he had had but the barest glimpse as he had stood in the doorway. As he had ushered Margaret out of his consulting-room he hadn't looked in her direction. All the same, it was interesting to have seen him again in his own environment, as it were. Very remote and professional, thought Mary Jane, eating a last sandwich, not a bit like the man who had pushed his way into her tea-room, demanding tea for his friend. She sighed for no reason at all, picked up a magazine and sat reading, a girl not worth a second glance, until it was time to go up to Margaret's room and warn her that dinner would be in half an hour.

Getting Margaret there by ten o'clock was rather an effort but she managed it, to be told by the nurse that Sir Thomas had been at one of the hospitals since the early hours of the morning operating on an emergency case. He would be with them as soon as possible and in the meantime perhaps they would like coffee?

'Well, this is really too bad,' grumbled Margaret. 'I am a private patient...'

'This was an emergency, Mrs Seymour,' said the nurse smoothly and went to get the coffee.

Mary Jane sat allowing Margaret's indignant whine to pass over her head. Like him or not, she felt sorry for Sir Thomas, up half the night and then having to cope with someone like Margaret instead of having a nap. She hoped he wouldn't be too tired...

When he came presently he looked exactly like a man who had enjoyed a good night's sleep, with time to dress with his usual elegance and eat a good breakfast. Only, when she peeped at him while he was greeting Margaret, she saw that there were tired lines around his eyes. He caught her staring at him when he turned to bid her good morning and she blushed a little. He watched the pretty colour pinken her cheeks and smiled. It was a kind and friendly smile and she was taken by surprise by it.

'Your patient? Was the operation successful?' She went even pinker; perhaps she shouldn't have asked— it wasn't any of her business.

'Entirely, thank you—a good start to my day.' Thank heaven he hadn't sounded annoyed, thought Mary Jane.

The nurse led Margaret away then, and Mary Jane sat and looked at the glossy magazines scattered around her. The models in them looked as though they should still be at school and were so thin that she longed to feed them up on good wholesome food. Some of the clothes were lovely but since she was never likely to wear any of them she took care not to want them too much.

I'm the wrong shape, she told herself, unaware that despite her thinness she had a pretty, curvy figure and nice legs, concealed by the tweed suit.

The door opened and Sir Thomas showed Margaret back into the waiting-room, and it was quite obvious that Margaret was in a dreadful temper whereas he presented an imperturbable manner. He didn't look at Mary Jane but shook Margaret's reluctant hand, wished her goodbye with cool courtesy and went back into his consulting-room.

Margaret took no notice of the nurse's polite goodbyes but flounced down to the street. 'I told you he was no good,' she hissed. 'The man's a fool, he says there is nothing wrong with me.' She gave a nasty little laugh. 'I'm to take more exercise, if you please— walk for an hour, mind you—each day, make beds, work in the garden, be active. I have suffered for years with my back, I'm quite unable to do anything strenuous; if you knew the hours I spend lying on the *chaise longue* ...'

'Perhaps that's why your back hurts,' suggested Mary Jane matter-of-factly.

'Don't be stupid. You can drive me home and I shall tell Dr Fellowes exactly what I think of him and his specialist.'

'He must know what he's talking about,' observed Mary Jane rashly, 'otherwise he wouldn't be a consultant, would he?'

'What do you know about it, anyway?' asked Margaret rudely. They had reached the hotel. 'Get your bag and get someone to bring the car round. We're leaving now.'

It was a pleasant autumn day; the drive would have been agreeable too if only Margaret would have stopped talking. Luckily she didn't need any answers, so Mary Jane was able to think her own thoughts.

She wasn't invited in when they arrived at the house. Mary Jane, to whom it had been home for happy years, hadn't expected that anyway. 'You can drive the car round to the garage before you go,' said Margaret without so much as a thank-you.

'Oliver can do that whenever he comes back; if you mind about it being parked outside you can drive it round yourself, Margaret; I'm going home.' She added rather naughtily, 'Don't forget that hour's walk each day.'

'Come back,' ordered Margaret. 'How can you be so cruel, leaving me like this?'

Mary Jane was already walking down the short drive. She called over her shoulder, 'But you're home, Margaret, and Sir Thomas said that there was nothing wrong with you...'

'I'll never speak to you again.'

'Oh, good.'

Mary Jane nipped smartly out of the open gate and down to the village. It was still mid-afternoon; she would open the tea-room in the hope that some passing motorist would fancy a pot of tea and scones. First she would have a meal; breakfast was hours ago and Margaret had refused to stop on the way. Beans on toast, she decided happily, opening her door.

Brimble was waiting for her, she picked him up and tucked him under an arm while she opened windows, turned the sign round to 'Open' and put the kettle on.

Brimble, content after a meal, sat beside her while she ate her own meal and then went upstairs to take a nap, leaving her to see that everything was ready for any customers who might come.

They came presently, much to her pleased surprise; a hiking couple, a family party in a car which looked as though it might fall apart at any moment and a married couple who quarrelled quietly all the while they ate their tea. Mary Jane locked the door with a feeling of satisfaction, got her supper and started on preparations for the next day. While she made a batch of tea-cakes she thought about Sir Thomas.

It was towards the end of October, on a chilly late afternoon, just as Mary Jane was thinking of closing since there was little likelihood of any customers, that Sir Thomas walked in. She had her back to the door, rearranging a shelf at the back of the tea-room and she had neither heard nor seen the Rolls come to a quiet halt outside.

'Too late for tea?' he asked and she spun round, clutching some plates.

'No—yes, I was just going to close.'

'Oh, good.' He turned the sign round. 'We can have a quiet talk without being disturbed.'

'Talk? Whatever about? Is something wrong with Miss Potter? I do hope not.'

'Miss Potter is making excellent progress...'

'Then it's Margaret—Mrs Seymour.'

'Ah, yes, the lady you escorted. As far as I know she is leading her normal life, and why not? There is nothing wrong with her. I came to talk about you.'

'Me. Why?'

'Put the kettle on and I'll tell you.'

Sir Thomas sat down at one of the little tables and ate one of the scones on a plate there, and, since it seemed that he intended to stay there until he had had his tea, Mary Jane put the plates down and went to put on the kettle.

By the time she came back with the teapot he had finished the scones and she fetched another plate, offering them wordlessly.

'You wanted to tell me something?' she prompted.

He sat back in the little cane chair so that it creaked alarmingly, his teacup in his hand. 'Yes...'

The thump on the door stopped him and when it was repeated he got up and unlocked it. The girl who came in flashed him a dazzling smile.

'Hello, Mary Jane. I'm on my way to Cheltenham and it seemed a good idea to look you up.' She pecked

Mary Jane's cheek and looked across at Sir Thomas. 'Am I interrupting something?'

'No,' said Mary Jane rather more loudly than necessary. 'This is Sir Thomas Latimer, an orthopaedic surgeon, he—that is, Margaret went to see him about her back and he has a patient in the village.' She glanced at him, still standing by the door. 'This is my sister, Felicity.'

Felicity was looking quite beautiful, of course; she dressed in the height of fashion and somehow the clothes always looked right on her. She had tinted her hair, too, and her make-up was exquisite, making the most of her dark eyes and the perfect oval of her face. She smiled at Sir Thomas now as he came to shake her hand, smiling down at her, holding her hand just a little longer than he need, making some easy light-hearted remark which made Felicity laugh.

Of course, he's fallen for her, reflected Mary Jane; since Felicity had left home to join the glamorous world of fashion she had had a continuous flow of men at her beck and call and she couldn't blame Sir Thomas; her sister was quite lovely. She said, 'Felicity is a well-known model...'

'I can't imagine her being anything else,' observed Sir Thomas gravely. 'Are you staying here with Mary Jane?'

'Lord, no. There's only one bedroom and I'd be terribly in the way—she gets up at the crack of dawn to cook, don't you, darling?' She glanced around her. 'Still making a living? Good. No, I'm booked in at the Queens at Cheltenham, I'm doing a dress show there tomorrow.' She smiled at Sir Thomas. 'I suppose you wouldn't like to come? We could have dinner...?'

'How delightful that would have been, although the dress show hardly appeals, but dinner with you would be another matter.'

The fool, thought Mary Jane fiercely. She had seen Felicity capture a man's attention a dozen times and not really minded but now she did. Sir Thomas was like the rest of them but for some reason she had thought that he was different.

Felicity gave an exaggerated sigh. 'Surely you could manage dinner? I don't know anyone in Cheltenham.'

'I'm on my way back to London,' he told her. 'Then I'm off to a seminar in Holland.'

Felicity said with a hint of sharpness, 'A busy man—are you a very successful specialist or something, making your millions?'

'I am a busy man, yes.' He smiled charmingly and she turned away to say goodbye to Mary Jane.

'Perhaps I'll drop in as I go back,' she suggested.

He opened the door for her and then walked with her to her car. Mary Jane could hear her sister's laughter before she drove away. She began to clear away the tea tray, she still had to do some baking ready for the next day and Brimble was prowling round, grumbling for his supper.

'We didn't finish our tea,' observed Sir Thomas mildly. He looked at her with questioning eyebrows.

Well, he is not getting another pot, reflected Mary Jane, and told him so, only politely. 'I've a lot of baking to do and I expect you want to get back to London.'

Sir Thomas's eyes gleamed with amusement. 'Then I won't keep you.' He picked up the coat he had tossed over a chair. 'You have a very beautiful sister, Mary Jane.'

'Yes, we're not a bit alike, are we?'

'No, not in the least.' A remark which did nothing to improve her temper. 'And I haven't had the opportunity to talk to you...'

'I don't suppose it was of the least importance.' She spoke tartly. 'You can tell me if we meet again, which isn't very likely.'

He opened the door. 'You are mistaken about a great many things, Mary Jane,' he told her gravely. 'Goodnight.'

She closed the door and bolted it and went back to the kitchen, not wishing to see him go.

She washed the cups and saucers with a good deal of noise, fed Brimble and got out the pastry board, the rolling pin and the ingredients for the scones. Her mind not being wholly on her work, her dough suffered a good deal of rough treatment; notwithstanding, the scones came from the oven nicely risen and golden brown. She cleared away and went upstairs, having lost all appetite for her supper.

Felicity hadn't said when she would come again but she seldom did, dropping in from time to time when it suited her. When they had been younger she had always treated Mary Jane with a kind of tolerant affection, at the same time making no effort to take much interest in her. It had been inevitable that Mary Jane should stay at home with her aunt and uncle and, even when they had died and she had inherited the cottage, Felicity had made no effort to help in any way. She was earning big money by then but neither she nor, for that matter, Mary Jane had expected her to do anything to make life easier for her young sister. Mary Jane had accepted the fact that Felicity was a success in life, leading a glamorous existence, travelling, picking and choosing for whom she would work and, while she was glad that she had made such a success of her life, she had no wish to be a part of it and certainly she felt no envy. Common sense told her that a plain face and a tendency to stay in the background would never earn her a place in the world of fashion.

Not that she would have liked that, she was content with her tea-room and Brimble and her friends in the village, although it would have been nice to have had a little more money.

The Misses Potter came in for their usual tea on the following day.

Miss Mabel was walking with a stick now and was a changed woman. They had been to Cheltenham on the previous day, they told Mary Jane, and that nice Sir Thomas had said that she need not go to see him anymore, just go for a check-up to Dr Fellowes every few months.

'He's going away,' she explained to Mary Jane, 'to some conference or other, but we heard that he will be going to the Radcliffe Infirmary at Oxford when he gets back. Much sought-after,' said Miss Mabel with satisfaction.

Of course, the village knew all about him calling at the tea-room and, Mary Jane being Mary Jane, her explanation that he had merely called for a cup of tea on his way back to London was accepted without comment. Felicity's visit had also been noticed with rather more interest. Very few people took *Vogue* or *Harpers and Queen* but those who visited their dentist or doctor and read the magazines in the waiting-room were well aware of her fame.

She came a few days later during the morning, walking into the tea-room and giving the customers there a pleasant surprise. She was wearing a suede outfit in red with boots in black leather and a good deal of gold jewellery. Not at all the kind of clothes the village was used to; even the doctor's wife and Margaret, not to mention the lady of the manor, wouldn't have risked wearing such an outfit. She smiled around her, confident that she was creating an impression.

'Hello, Mary Jane,' she said smilingly, pleased with the mild sensation she had caused. 'Can you spare me a cup of coffee? I'm on my way back to town.'

She sat down at one of the tables and Mary Jane, busy with serving, said, 'Hello, Felicity. Yes, of course, but will you help yourself? I'm quite busy.'

The customers went presently, leaving the two sisters alone. Mary Jane collected up cups and saucers and tidied the tables and Felicity said rather impatiently, 'Oh, do sit down for a minute, you can wash up after I've gone.'

Mary Jane fetched a cup of coffee for herself, refilled Felicity's cup and sat. 'Did you have a successful show?' she asked.

'Marvellous. I'm off to the Bahamas next week—*Vogue* and *Elle*. When I get back it will be time for the dress show in Paris. Life's all go...'

'Would you like to change it?'

Felicity gave her a surprised stare. 'Change it? My dear girl, have you any idea of the money I earn?'

'Well no, I don't think that I have...' Mary Jane spoke without rancour. 'But it must be a great deal.'

'It is. I like money and I spend it. In a year or two I intend to find a wealthy husband and settle down.

Sooner, if I meet someone I fancy.' She smiled across the little table. 'Like that man I met when I was here last week. Driving a Rolls and doing very nicely and just my type. I can't think how you met him, Mary Jane.'

'He operated on a friend of mine here and I met him at the hospital. He stopped for a cup of tea on his way back to London. I don't know anything about him except that he's a specialist in bones.'

'How revolting.' Felicity wrinkled her beautiful nose. 'But of course, he must have a social life. Is he married?'

'I've no idea. I should think it must be very likely, wouldn't you?'

'London, you say? I must find out. What's his name?'

Mary Jane told her but with reluctance. There was no reason why she should mind Felicity's interest in him, indeed she would make a splendid foil for his magnificent size and good looks and presumably he would be able to give Felicity all the luxury she demanded of life.

'He said he was going abroad—to Holland, I think,' she volunteered.

'Good. That gives me time to track him down. Once I know where he lives or works I can meet him again—accidentally of course.'

Well, thought Mary Jane in her sensible way, he's old enough and wise enough to look after himself and there's that other woman who came here with him . . .

She didn't mention her to her sister.

Felicity didn't stay long. 'Ticking over nicely?' she asked carelessly. 'You always liked a quiet life, didn't you?'

What would Felicity have said if she had declared that she would very much like to wear lovely clothes, go dancing and be surrounded by young men? Mary Jane, loading a tray carefully, agreed placidly.

Since it seemed likely that the quiet life was to be her lot, there wasn't much point in saying anything else.

CHAPTER THREE

OCTOBER, sliding towards November, had turned wet and chilly and customers were sparse. Mary Jane turned out cupboards, washed and polished and cut down on the baking. There were still customers glad of a cup of tea, home from shopping expeditions—or motorists on their way to Cheltenham or Oxford stopped for coffee. More prosperous tea-rooms closed down during the winter months and their owners went to Barbados or California to spend their summer's profits, but Mary Jane's profits weren't large enough for that. Besides, since she lived over the tea-room she might just as well keep it open and get what custom there was.

On this particular morning, since it was raining hard and moreover was a Monday, she was pleased to hear the doorbell tinkle as she set the percolator on the stove. It wasn't a customer, though. Oliver stood there, just inside the door.

She wasn't particularly pleased to see him but she wished him a cheerful good morning.

'I'm just back from the States,' declared Oliver pompously. 'Margaret tells me that you have behaved most unkindly towards her. I should have thought that you could at least have stayed with her and made sure that she was quite comfortable.'

'But she is not ill—Sir Thomas Latimer said so. He said that she should take more exercise and not lie around.'

Oliver's eyes bulged with annoyance. 'I consider you to be a heartless girl, Mary Jane. I shall think twice before asking you to do any small favour...'

'You'd be wasting time,' said Mary Jane matter-of-factly, 'for you're quite able to find someone else if Margaret insists on feeling poorly all the time. I've my living to earn, you know.'

Oliver's eyes slid away from hers. 'As a matter of fact, I have to go away again very shortly...'

'Then you can arrange for someone to be with Margaret; don't waste your time with me, Oliver.'

'You ungrateful...'

She came and stood before him. 'Tell me, what am I ungrateful for?' she invited.

Oliver still didn't meet her eyes. 'Well,' he began.

'Just so, go away, Oliver, before I bang you over the head with my rolling pin.'

'Don't be ridiculous,' he blustered. All the same he edged towards the door.

Which opened to admit the giant-like person of Sir Thomas, his elegant grey suit spattered with rain. He said nothing, only stood there, his eyebrows slightly raised, smiling a little.

Mary Jane had gone pink at the sight of him; blushing was a silly habit she had never quite conquered. She was pleased to see him. Oliver, after a first startled glance, had ignored him. 'You've not heard the last of this, Mary Jane—your own flesh and blood.'

'Ah,' said Sir Thomas, in the gentlest of voices. 'You are, I believe, Mrs Seymour's husband?'

Oliver goggled. 'Yes—yes, I am.' He puffed out his chest in readiness for a few well-chosen words but he was forestalled.

'Delighted to meet you,' said Sir Thomas with suave untruthfulness. 'It gives me the opportunity to tell you that there is nothing wrong with your wife. A change of lifestyle is all that she needs—rather more activity.'

Oliver looked from him to Mary Jane who in her turn was studying the row of glass jars on the shelf on the further wall. 'Really, surely this is hardly the place,' he began.

'Oh, Miss Seymour was with your wife and of course already knows what I have told Mrs Seymour. I thought it might reassure you to mention it. You will, of course, get a report from your own doctor in due course.'

He opened the door invitingly, letting in a good deal of wind and rain, and Oliver, muttering that he was a busy man, hurried out to his car without a word more than a cursory good morning.

Sir Thomas brushed a few drops of rain off his sleeve and Mary Jane said, 'You're wet.'

He glanced at her. 'I was passing in the car and saw you talking to your—cousin? You looked as though you were going to hit him and it seemed a good idea to—er—join you.'

'I threatened him with a rolling pin,' said Mary Jane in a satisfied voice.

'Admirable. A very handy weapon. Do you often use it?' He added gravely, 'As a weapon?'

'Well, of course not. He was annoying me. Do you want coffee?'

'I was hoping that you would ask me. And are there any scones?'

She set a plate on the table and a dish of butter and he spread a scone and bit into it.

'Are you hungry?' asked Mary Jane pointedly.

'Famished. I've been at the Radcliffe all night...'

She poured coffee for them both and sat down opposite him. 'But you're going the wrong way home.'

'Ah, yes. I thought I'd take a day off. I've a clinic at six o'clock this evening. It crossed my mind that it would be pleasant if we were to spend it together. Lunch perhaps? A drive through the countryside?'

'Oughtn't you to go to bed?'

'If you were to offer me a boiled egg or even a rasher or two of bacon I'll doze for ten minutes or so while you do whatever it is you do before you go out for the day.'

'The tea-room...'

'Just for once?' He contrived to look hungry and lonely, although she suspected that he was neither.

'Bacon and eggs,' she told him before she could change her mind. 'And I'll need half an hour.'

'Excellent. I'll come and watch you cook.'

He sat on the kitchen table, Brimble on his knee, while she got out the frying pan and, while the bacon sizzled, sliced bread and made more coffee.

'Two eggs?' She looked up and found him staring at her. It was a thoughtful look and she wondered about it until he spoke.

'Yes, please. Where is your beautiful sister, Mary Jane?'

She cracked the eggs neatly. For some reason his question had made her unhappy although she had no intention of letting it show. 'Well, she went to Barbados but she should be back by now—I think it's the Paris dress shows next week. She lives in London, though. Would you like to have her address?'

'Yes, please, I feel I owe her a dinner. If you remember?'

'Yes, of course.' She wrote on the back of the pad, tore off the page and gave it to him. 'That's her phone number, too.'

She didn't look at him but dished up his breakfast and fetched the coffee-pot.

'I'll go and change while you eat,' she told him. 'Brimble likes the bacon rinds.'

Upstairs she inspected her wardrobe. It would have to be the jersey dress, kept for unlikely occasions such as this one, and the Marks and Spencer mac. Somewhere or other there was a rainproof hat—if only she had the sort of curly hair which looked enchanting when it got wet...

She went downstairs presently and found Sir Thomas, his chair balanced precariously against the wall, his large feet on the table, asleep. He had tidied his breakfast plate away into the sink and Brimble, licking the last of the bacon rinds from his whiskers, was perched on his knees.

Mary Jane stood irresolute. It would be cruel to wake him up; on the other hand he looked very uncomfortable.

'A splendid breakfast,' said Sir Thomas, his eyes still closed. 'I feel like a new man.'

He opened his eyes then. No one would have known that he had been up all night.

'Have you really been up all night?' asked Mary Jane. She blinked at the sudden cold stare.

'I have many faults, but I don't lie.' His voice was as cold as his eyes and she made haste to make amends.

'I'm sorry, I wasn't doubting you, only you look so—so tidy!' she finished lamely.

'Tidy? I have showered and shaved and put on a clean shirt. Is that being tidy?' He lifted Brimble gently from his knee and stood up, towering over her. His gaze swept over her person. 'Most suitably dressed for the weather,' he observed, and she bore his scrutiny silently, aware that the hat, while practical, did nothing for her at all.

She turned the sign to 'Closed', coaxed Brimble into his basket, shut windows and locked doors and pronounced herself ready. The rain was still sheeting down. 'You'll get wet,' she told him. 'I've an umbrella ...'

He smiled and took the key from her and locked the tea-room door and went to unlock the car door, bundled her in, gave himself a shake and got in beside her. 'Oxford?' he asked and, when she nodded happily, smiled.

Mary Jane, suddenly shy, was relieved when he started an undemanding conversation, and he, versed in the art of putting people at their ease, kept up a flow of small talk until they reached Oxford. The rain had eased a little, and, with the car safely parked, they set out on a walk around the colleges.

'Did you come here?' asked Mary Jane, craning her neck to see Tom Tower.

'I was at Trinity.'

'Before you trained as a doctor—no, surgeon.'

'I took my MD, and then went over to surgery—orthopaedics.'

She lowered her gaze from Tom Tower to her companion. 'I expect you're very clever.'

'Everyone is clever at something,' he told her, and took her arm and walked her to the Radcliffe Camera.

'May we go inside?'

'To the reading rooms if you like. It houses the Bodleian Library.'

He took her to the Eastgate Hotel and gave her coffee in the bar, a cheerful place, crowded with students, and then walked her briskly down to the river before popping her back into the car.

'There's a rather nice place for lunch,' he told her casually, 'a few miles away.'

An understatement, Mary Jane decided when they reached Le Manoir aux Quat' Saisons at Great Milton; it was definitely a grand place and the jersey dress was quite inadequate. However, she was given no time to worry about that. She was whisked inside, led away to tidy herself and then settled in the bar with a glass of sherry while Sir Thomas, very much at his ease, sat opposite her studying the menu. He glanced at her presently.

'Dublin Bay prawns?' he suggested. 'And what about *poulet Normand*?'

Mary Jane agreed, she had never tasted Dublin Bay prawns but she was hungry enough to try anything; as for the chicken, she had read the recipe for that in her cookery book—egg yolks and thick cream and brandy, butter and onions—it sounded delicious.

It was. She washed it down with spa water and, when invited, chose an orange cream soufflé—more cream, and Curaçao this time. Over coffee she said, in her sensible way, 'This is a delightful place and that was the most gorgeous meal I've had for a long time. You're very kind.'

She caught his eye and went a little pink. 'Oh, dear, I've made it sound like a half-term treat with an...' She stopped just in time and the pink deepened.

'Uncle? Godfather?' he suggested, and she let out a sigh of relief when he laughed. 'I've enjoyed my day too, Mary Jane, you are a very restful companion; you haven't rearranged your hair once or powdered your nose or put on more lipstick and you really enjoyed Oxford, didn't you?'

'Oh, very much. It's a long time since I was there.' She fell silent, remembering how her father used to take Felicity and her there, walking the streets, pointing out the lovely old buildings, and Sir Thomas watched her with faint amusement and vague pity. So independent, he reflected, making a life for herself, and so different from her rather beautiful sister. He must remember to mention her funny little tea-room to his family and friends; drum up some customers for her so that she would have some money to spend on herself. A new hat for a start. No rain hat was becoming but at least it need not be quite as awful as the one she had been wearing all day.

Her quiet voice interrupted his thoughts. 'If you are to be back in London this evening ought we not to be going? I don't want to go,' she added childishly and smiled at him, her violet eyes glowing because she was happy.

'I don't want to go either, but you are quite right.' He had uttered the words almost without thinking and realised to his surprise that he had meant them; he had really enjoyed her company, undemanding, ready to be pleased with everything they had seen and done.

He drove her back to the tea-room, talking about nothing much, at ease with each other, but when she offered him tea he refused. 'I've played truant for long enough. It has been a delightful day, Mary Jane— thank you for your company.'

She offered a small gloved hand. 'Thank you for asking me. It was a treat and so much nicer because I hadn't expected one. I hope you're not too busy this evening so that you can get a good night's sleep, Sir Thomas.'

He concealed a smile. The evening clinic was always busy and there was a pile of work awaiting him on his desk at home.

'I have no doubt of it,' he told her cheerfully, and got into his car and drove away.

She stood at the door until he was out of sight and then took off her outdoor things, fed a peevish Brimble and put the kettle on. It had been a lovely day; she thought about it, minute by minute, while she sipped her tea. She had too much common sense to suppose that Sir Thomas had actually wished for her company—he had needed a companion to share his day and she had been handy and it was obvious that he had called that morning so that he might get Felicity's address. His invitation had been on the spur of the moment and she was quite sure that she fell far short of his usual companions. And she had seen the look he had cast at the rain hat. She got up and went to examine her face in the small looking glass on the kitchen wall. It was rosy from her day out of doors but she didn't see how her skin glowed with health and how her eyes shone. All she saw was her hair, damp around the edges where it had escaped from the hat, and the lack of make-up.

'You're a plain girl,' she told her reflection, and Brimble looked up from his grooming to mutter an agreement.

Promptly at six o'clock, Sir Thomas sat himself down behind his desk in the clinic consultation-room and listened patiently as one patient after the other took the seat opposite to him, to be led away in turn to be carefully examined by him, and then told, in the kindest possible way, what was wrong and what would have to be done. It was almost nine o'clock by the time the last patient had been shown out and he and his registrar and houseman prepared to leave too. Outpatients Sister stifled a yawn as she collected notes—she hated the evening clinic but she had worked with Sir Thomas for several years now and if he had decided to have a clinic at three o'clock in the morning, she would have agreed cheerfully. He was her—and almost all of the nursing staff's—ideal man, never hurried, always polite, unfailingly patient, apparently unaware of the devotion accorded him. For such a successful man he was singularly unconceited.

He bade everyone goodnight and drove himself to his home; a house in a row of similar elegant houses in Little Venice, facing the Grand Union Canal. It had stopped raining at last and the late evening was quiet. He opened his front door and as he did so an elderly man, rather stout and short, came into the hall.

'Evening, Tremble,' said Sir Thomas, and tossed his coat on to an elbow chair beside a Georgian mahogany side-table.

Tremble picked up the coat and folded it carefully over one arm. 'Good evening, sir. Mrs Tremble has a nice little dinner all ready for you.'

'Thank you.' Sir Thomas was looking through his post. 'Give me ten minutes, will you?'

He took his post and his bag into the study at the back of the hall and sat down to read the letters before going up to his room, to return presently and sit by the fire in the big drawing-room at the front of the house. He was greeted here by a Labrador dog, who got to elderly feet and lumbered happily to meet him.

Sir Thomas sat down, a glass of whisky beside him, the dog's head on his knee. 'A pity you weren't with us, old fellow,' he said. 'I rather fancy you would have liked her.'

Tremble's voice reminded him that dinner was served and he crossed the hall with the dog to the dining-room, a room beautifully furnished with a Regency mahogany twin pedestal table surrounded by Hepplewhite chairs; there was an inlaid mahogany sideboard of the same period against one wall and the lighting was pleasantly subdued from the brass sconces on the walls. There were paintings too—Dutch flower studies and a number of portraits.

Sir Thomas, being a very large man, ate his dinner with good appetite, exchanging a casual conversation with Tremble as he was served and offering his dog the last morsel of his cheese.

'Watson had his supper an hour ago, sir,' said Tremble severely.

'We are told that cheese is good for the digestion, Tremble; I suppose that applies to dogs as well as humans.'

'I really couldn't say, sir. Will you have your coffee in the drawing-room?'

'Please, and do tell Mrs Tremble that everything was delicious.'

He went to his study presently with Watson as company, and worked at his desk. He had quite forgotten Mary Jane.

Even if Mary Jane had wanted to forget him she wasn't given that chance. Naturally, in a village that size, she had been seen getting into Sir Thomas's Rolls-Royce, a news item flashed round the village in no time at all, so that when she got out of it again that late afternoon, several ladies living in the cottages on either side of her saw that too.

Trade was brisk the following morning and it was only after she had answered a few oblique questions that she realised why. Since some of the ladies in the tea-room were prone to embroider any titbit of news to make it more exciting, she told them about her day out in a sensible manner which revealed not a whiff of romance.

She was well-liked; disappointed as they were at her prosaic description of her day with Sir Thomas, they were pleased that she had enjoyed herself. She had little enough fun and no opportunity of getting away from the village and meeting young people of her own age. They lingered over their coffee and, when the Misses Potter joined them, the talk turned, naturally enough, to Sir Thomas.

'Such a nice man,' declared Miss Mabel. 'As mild as milk.'

'Even milk boils over from time to time,' muttered Mary Jane, offering a plate of digestive biscuits, the scones had all been eaten long-since.

Sir Thomas, arriving at his consulting-rooms in Wigmore Street the following morning, wished Miss Pink, his secretary and receptionist, a cheerful good morning and paused at her desk.

'What have I got this weekend?' he wanted to know.

'You're making a speech at that dinner on Saturday evening. Miss Thorley phoned and asked would you like to take her to dinner on Sunday evening; she suggested a day out somewhere first.' Miss Pink's voice was dry.

For a moment Mary Jane's happy face, crowned with the deplorable hat, floated before Sir Thomas's eyes. He said at once, 'I intend to go down to my mother's. Would you phone Miss Thorley and tell her I shall be away?'

Miss Pink gave him a thoughtful look and he returned it blandly. 'I'm far too busy to phone her myself.'

Miss Pink allowed herself a gentle smile as Sir Thomas went into his consulting-room; Miss Thorley, on the rare occasions when she had seen her, had looked at her as though she despised her and Miss Pink, of no discernible age, sharp-nosed and spectacled, objected strongly to that.

There was just time before the first patient was announced for Sir Thomas to phone his mother and invite himself for the weekend.

Her elderly, comfortable voice came clearly over the wires. 'How nice, dear. Are you bringing anyone with you?'

He said that no, he wasn't and the fleeting thought that it would be interesting to see his mother and Mary Jane together whisked through his head, to be instantly dismissed as so much nonsense.

Mary Jane's day out, while not exactly a nine-day wonder, kept the village interested for a few days until the local postman's daughter's wedding. An event which caused the village to turn out *en masse* to crowd into the church and throw confetti afterwards. It brought some welcome custom to Mary Jane, too, for somewhere was needed afterwards where the details of the wedding, the bride's finery and speculation as to the happy couple's future happiness could be mulled over. She did a roaring trade in coffee and scones and, for latecomers, sausage rolls.

She went to bed that night confident that, with luck, she would be able to get a new winter coat.

It was almost midnight by the time Sir Thomas, resplendent in white tie and tails, returned from the banquet which he had been invited to attend. He had made his speech, brief and to the point, and it had been well received and now it was just a question of changing into comfortable clothes, collecting a sleepy Watson and getting into his car once more. It would be late by the time he reached his mother's house, but he had a key. At that time of night, with the roads quiet and a good deal of them motorway, he should be there in little over an hour.

Which he was; he slowed down as he entered the village, its inhabitants long since in bed, and took the car slowly past the church and then, a few hundred yards further, through the open gates of the house beyond.

The night was chilly with a hint of frost and there was bright moonlight. The low, rambling house was in darkness save for a dim light shining through the transom over the door. Sir Thomas got out quietly, opened the door for Watson and stood for a moment while his companion trotted off into the shrubbery at the side of the house, to reappear shortly and, as silent as his master, enter the house.

The hall was square, low-ceilinged and pleasantly warm. There was a note by the lamp on the side-table. Someone had printed 'Coffee on the Aga' on a card and propped it against the elegant china base of the lamp. Sir Thomas smiled a little and went soft-footed to the baize door beside the staircase and so through to the kitchen door where he poured his coffee, gave Watson a drink and presently took himself up to his bed, leaving Watson already asleep on the rug before the Aga.

Four hours later he was up and dressed, drinking tea in the kitchen and talking to his mother's housekeeper, Mrs Beaver.

'And how's that nasty old London?' she wanted to know.

'Well, I don't see a great deal of it, I spend most of my days either at the hospital or my rooms. I often wonder why I don't resign and come and live in peace and quiet here.'

'Go on with you, Sir Thomas, leaving that clever brain of yours to moulder away doing nothing but walking the dog and shooting pigeons. That's not you. Now if you was to ask me, I'd say get yourself a wife and a clutch of children—no question of you giving up then with all them mouths to feed.'

He put down his mug and gave her a hug, 'You old matchmaker,' he told her, and whistled to Watson. It was a fine, chilly morning; there was time to go for a walk before breakfast.

His mother was at the table when he got back, sitting behind the coffee pot; a small, slim woman with pepper and salt hair done in an old-fashioned bun and wearing a beautifully tailored suit.

'There you are, Thomas. How nice to see you, dear, I suppose you can't stay for a few days?'

He bent to kiss her. 'Afraid not, Mama—I'm rather booked up for the next week or so, I'll have to go back very early on Monday morning.'

He helped himself to bacon and eggs, added mushrooms and a tomato or two and sat down beside her. 'The garden looks pretty good...'

'Old Dodds knows his job, though he's a bit pernickety when I want to cut some flowers.' She handed him his coffee, 'Well, what have you been doing, my dear—other than work?'

'Nothing much. A banquet I couldn't miss yesterday evening and one or two dinner parties...'

'What happened to that gorgeous young woman who had begged a lift from you—oh, some weeks ago now?'

He speared a morsel of bacon and topped it neatly with a mushroom.

'Ingrid Bennett. I have no idea.' He smiled suddenly, remembering. 'She insisted on stopping for tea and we did, at a funny little tea-room in a village near Stow-on-the-Wold, run by a small tartar with a sharp tongue.'

'Pretty?'

'No. A great deal of mousy hair and violet eyes.'

His mother buttered toast. 'How unusual—I mean the eyes. One never knows the hidden delights of remote villages until one has a reason to go to them.' She peeped at him and found him watching her, smiling.

'She interested you?'

'As a person? Perhaps; she was so unlike the elegant young women I usually meet socially. But more than that, I imagine she scratches a bare living from the place and yet she seemed quite content with her lot.'

'No family?'

'A sister. A beautiful creature—a top model, flitting about the world and making a great deal of money, I should imagine.'

'Then she might give something to the tea-shop owner.'

Sir Thomas reached for the marmalade. 'Somehow, I don't think that has occurred to her. Do we have to go to church?'

'Of course. We will have a lovely afternoon reading the Sunday papers and having tea round the fire.'

Mary Jane, always hopeful of customers even on a Monday morning, was taking the first batch of teacakes from the oven when the doorbell rang. She glanced at the clock on the wall; half-past eight and she hadn't even turned the sign round to 'Open' yet. Perhaps it was the postman with a parcel...

Sir Thomas was standing with his back to the door, his hands in his pockets, but he turned round as she unlocked the door and opened it.

She would have turned the sign round too but he put a large hand over hers to prevent that. 'Good morning, Mary Jane. May I beg a cup of coffee from you? I know it's still early.' He sounded meek, not at all as he usually spoke and she jumped at once to the wrong conclusion as he had anticipated.

'You're on your way back to London? You've been up all night?'

Her lovely eyes were soft with sympathy. She didn't wait for an answer, which saved him from perjury, but went on briskly. 'Well, come on in. Coffee won't take more than a few minutes—I could make you some toast . . .'

'Something smells very appetising.' He followed her into the kitchen.

'Teacakes. I've just made some.' She looked at him over her shoulder. 'Do you want one?'

'Indeed I do.' He wandered back to the door. 'I have my dog with me. Might he come in? Would Brimble object?'

'A dog?' She looked surprised. 'Of course he can come in. Brimble isn't up yet, but I'll shut the stairs door anyway.'

Watson, his nose twitching at the prospect of something to eat, greeted her with gentle dignity. 'Whenever possible he goes everywhere with me,' said Sir Thomas.

Mary Jane fetched a bowl and filled it with water and offered a digestive biscuit. 'The poor lamb, he'll be glad to get home, I expect.' She added shyly, 'You too, Sir Thomas.'

'I'll drop him off before I go to my rooms.'

She poured his coffee, offered a plate of buttered tea-cakes and poured coffee for herself. 'But you'll have to have some rest—you can't possibly do a day's work if you've been up all night. You might make a wrong diagnosis.'

Sir Thomas swallowed a laugh. He should, he reflected, be feeling guilty at his deception, actually he was enjoying himself immensely.

Over his second cup of coffee he asked, 'How's business? And is that cousin of yours bothering you?'

'I make a living,' she told him seriously. 'Oliver hasn't been again—I think that was the second time I've seen him in years. He isn't likely to come again.'

'No other family?' he asked casually.

'No—there's just Felicity and me. He quite likes her though because she's quite famous.'

'And you, Mary Jane, have you no wish to be famous?'

'Me? Famous? What could I be famous for? And I wouldn't want to be, anyway.' She added with a touch of defiance, 'I am very happy here. I've got Brimble and I know almost everyone in the village.'

'You don't wish to marry?'

She got up to refill his cup. 'I've not met many men—not in a village as small as this one. It would be nice to marry but it would have to be someone I—I loved. Could you eat another teacake?'

'I could, but I won't. I must be on my way.'

She watched him drive away, Watson sitting beside him, and went back to make more teacakes and fresh coffee. She didn't expect to be busy on a Monday morning but it was nice to be prepared.

As it turned out, she had several customers; early though it was and after a brief lull the Misses Potter came—most unusually for them on a Monday, to tell her over coffee that their nephew from Canada would be coming to visit them. They in their turn were followed by Mrs Fellowes, to ask her over still more coffee if she would babysit for them on the following Saturday as Dr Fellowes had got tickets for the theatre in Cheltenham. Mary Jane agreed cheerfully; the doctor's children were small and cuddly and once they were asleep they needed very little attention. Mrs Fellowes had been gone only a few moments before two cars stopped, disgorging children and parents and what looked like Granny and Grandpa. They ate all the teacakes and most of the scones, drank a gratifying amount of coffee and lemonade and went away again with noisy cheerfulness, leaving her to clear away, close the tea-room for the lunch-hour and, after a quick sandwich, start on another batch of scones.

No one came during the early afternoon and in a way she was glad for it gave her time to return everything to its usual pristine order. It was almost four o'clock and she was wondering if she should close for the day when a car drew up and a lady got out, opened the door and asked if she might have tea.

'Have a table by the window,' invited Mary Jane. 'It's a nice afternoon and I like this time of day, don't you? Indian or China, and would you like scones or teacakes?'

'China and scones, please. What a charming village.' The lady smiled at her and Mary Jane smiled back; her customer wasn't young but she was dressed in the kind of tweeds Mary Jane would have liked to be able to afford and her pepper and salt hair was stylishly dressed. She had a very kind face, full of laughter lines.

Mary Jane brought the tea and a plate of scones, butter and a dish of strawberry jam, and Sir Thomas's mother engaged her in idle talk while she studied her. So this was the girl with the violet eyes; the tartar with a sharp tongue. She approved of what she saw and the eyes were certainly startlingly lovely.

'I don't suppose you get many customers at this time of year?' she asked casually.

'Well, no, although today I've been quite busy...'

'You don't open until mid-morning, I suppose,' asked Mrs Latimer, following a train of thought.

'About nine o'clock—I opened early today, though—someone who had been up all night and needed a hot drink.'

Mary Jane's cheeks went nicely pink at the thought of Sir Thomas. To cover her sudden confusion at the thought of him, she went on lightly, 'He had a dog with him—he was called Watson...'

'What an unusual name,' said Mrs Latimer, and silently congratulated herself on her maternal instincts. 'For a dog, I mean. What delicious scones.' She smiled at Mary Jane. 'I am so glad I came here.'

CHAPTER FOUR

THE evenings were closing in and the mornings were crisp. Mary Jane, locking the door after another day almost devoid of customers, thought of Felicity in London from whom she had had a card that morning. The Paris show had been a resounding success and she was having a few days off before another week or so of modelling, this time in the Seychelles. Mary Jane, reading it without envy, wondered why they had to go so far to take photos of clothes which only a tiny percentage of women wore. She wondered who paid for it all—perhaps that was why the clothes were so wildly expensive.

She fed Brimble, had her supper and spent the evening shortening the hem of the jersey dress. Short skirts were the fashion and she had nice legs even if there was no one to notice that.

The morning brought several customers, the last of whom, an elderly man, looked so ill she gave him a second cup of coffee without charging for it. He had a dreadful cough, too, watering eyes and a face as white as paper.

As he got up to go she said diffidently, 'You have got a frightful cold; should you be out?'

'Got a job to do,' he said hoarsely. 'No good giving in, miss.'

Poor fellow, thought Mary Jane, and then forgot him. Closing up for the day later, she peered out into

the cold, wet evening and thought with sympathy of
Dr and Mrs Fellowes who had gone to London for a
few days. It was no weather for a holiday.

She woke up in the night with a sore throat and
when she got up she had a headache. There were no
customers all day and for once she was glad because
she was beginning to feel peculiar. She closed early,
locking the door thankfully against persistent rain and
a rising wind and, since she wasn't hungry, she fed
Brimble, made herself a hot drink and went to bed
after a hot bath, but even its warmth and that of the
hot water bottle she clasped to her made no difference
to the icy shivers running down her spine. Brimble,
that most understanding of cats, got on to the bed
presently and stretched out against her and soon she
slept, fitfully, relieved when it was morning. A cup
of tea teamed with a couple of Panadol would make
her feel better. She crept downstairs, gave Brimble his
breakfast, drank her tea and went back to bed. The
weather had worsened during the night and there was
no one about; there would certainly be no customers.
She went to sleep again, to wake every few hours with
a blinding headache and a chest which hurt when she
breathed. It was late afternoon when she crawled out
of bed again to feed Brimble, wash her face and put
on a clean nightie. A night's sleep would surely get
her back on her feet, she thought. She ought to make
herself a drink, but the very idea of going downstairs
again made her feel ill. She got back into bed ...

She woke several times aware that she was thirsty,
that she should feed Brimble, put on some clothes
and knock on Mrs Adams's door and get her to ask
Dr Fellowes' locum to come, but somehow she
couldn't be bothered to do anything about things. She

was dimly aware that Brimble was mewing but she was by now so muddled that she quite thought she had been downstairs to put out his food. She fell into an uneasy doze, not heeding the rain and the wind rattling at the windows.

Sir Thomas, driving himself back from a consultation in Bristol, turned off the motorway at Swindon. He would have to stop for lunch somewhere and he might as well go a little out of his way and have it at Mary Jane's. He had no appointments for the rest of the day and driving was tiring in the appalling weather. It was more than a little out of his way; from the village he would have to drive to Oxford but he had reasoned that he could pick up the M40 there, a mere fifty miles or so from London.

It was just after one o'clock when he stopped at the tea-room. There was no one around and no traffic, not that there was ever very much of that and he wasn't surprised to see the 'Closed' sign on the door. Mary Jane would be having her lunch. He got out of the car and went to the door and rang the bell and, since no one came, peered into the little room. Brimble was sitting on the little counter at the back, looking anxious, and when Sir Thomas tapped on the glass he jumped down and came to the door, standing on his hind legs, mewing urgently.

Sir Thomas rang again and knocked for good measure, standing patiently in his Burberry, the rain drenching his head. He stood back from the door and looked up to the windows above but there was no sign of anyone and after a moment he walked to the end of the little terrace and went down the narrow alley which led to the back gardens. Mary Jane's cottage was halfway along, he opened the flimsy gate, crossed the small garden and went to peer through the kitchen window. The kitchen was untidy, not at all in its usual state with a pan full of milk on the stove and the kettle and dishes and cutlery lying around. As he looked, Brimble jumped on to the draining board by the sink and scratched at the window, which, since he had his own cat-flap, seemed unnecessary. The cottages on either side were unlit and silent; Sir Thomas took out his Swiss Army penknife, selected one of its versatile components and eased it into the window frame.

The window opened easily for the hasp was loose, and he swung it wide so that Brimble might go out. He didn't want to. Instead he jumped down and went to the door leading to the stairs standing half-open.

Sir Thomas took off his Burberry, threw it into the kitchen and squeezed through the window, no easy task for a man of his splendid size. He gained the floor and stood for a moment, listening. When he called, 'Mary Jane,' in a quiet voice, there was silence and he started up the narrow little stairs.

As he reached the tiny landing Mary Jane came wobbling out of the bedroom. She was barefoot and in her nightie and her hair hung down her back and over her shoulders in an appalling tangle. Her pinched face was a nasty colour and her eyelids puffy. Not a pretty sight.

'Oh, it's you,' she said in a hoarse whisper.

Sir Thomas bit back strong language, scooped her up and laid her back in the tumbled bedclothes. She was in no state to answer questions; he went back downstairs, out of the door this time, fetched his bag from the car, paused long enough to fill Brimble's bowl with what he took to be cold milk-pudding in the top of the fridge and took the stairs two at a time.

Mary Jane hadn't moved but she opened her eyes as he sat down on the side of the bed. She was too weary to speak, which was just as well, for he popped a thermometer under her tongue and took her wrist in his large cool hand. It felt comforting and she curled her hot fingers round it and closed her eyes again.

Her temperature was high and her breaths rapid and so was her pulse. He said with reassuring calm, 'You have a nasty bout of flu, Mary Jane. Who's your doctor?'

She opened an eye. 'He's away.'

'Is there anyone to look after you?'

She frowned, not wanting to bother to answer him. 'No.'

He tucked her in firmly. 'I'll be back,' he told her and went out of the back door again and round to the front, to bang on the doors on either side of the tea-room. No one came to answer his thumps and he went to his car and picked up the phone.

Back in the cottage he set to work with quiet speed, clearing the kitchen, shutting and locking the kitchen door, fastening the window and then going upstairs again to fetch his bag. Mary Jane opened her eyes once more. 'Do go away,' she begged. 'I've such a headache.'

'You'll feel better presently,' he assured her, and then asked, 'Have you a box or basket for Brimble?'

'On top of the wardrobe.' She sat up suddenly. 'Why? He's all right, he's not ill?'

'No, but you are. I'm taking you to someone who will look after you both for a day or two. Now be a good girl and stay quiet until I get organised.'

Brimble wasn't pleased to be stuffed gently into his basket, but the hands which picked him up and stowed him away were gentle and he had been easily mellowed by the milk-pudding. He was borne into the tea-room and the basket put on top of one of the tables, next to the bag Sir Thomas had brought downstairs. He unlocked the shop door next and went back upstairs, rolled Mary Jane in the quilt and carried her downstairs. The stairs, being narrow, made things a bit difficult, but Mary Jane was small and slight even if the quilt was bulky. He opened the tea-room door and with some difficulty the car door and arranged his bundle beside his seat, strapped her in and went back for Brimble and his bag before locking the door of the tea-room. He was very wet by now since he hadn't bothered to put his Burberry on again but thrown it into the back of the car, but before he got into the car he stood a moment looking up and down the street. There was no sign of anyone; presumably everyone was indoors, sitting cosily by the fire, no doubt with the TV on very loud to drown the sound of the wind and the rain. He got in, gave a quick look at Mary Jane's sickly face and drove off.

After a minute or so Mary Jane opened her eyes. She felt very ill but she knew vaguely that there were some things she needed to know.

'Not hospital,' she muttered. 'Brimble . . .'

'Don't fuss,' advised Sir Thomas. 'You're going somewhere so that you can lie in bed for a day or two and get well, and Brimble will be right by you.'

'Oh, good,' said Mary Jane, and, remembering her manners, 'thank you, so sorry to be such a nuisance.'

She dozed off, lulled by his grunt, a reassuring commonplace sound which soothed her. She stirred only slightly when he stopped before his mother's front door and lifted her out as though she had been a bundle of feathers and carried her in. Mrs Latimer, waiting in the hall, took one look at Mary Jane. 'Oh, the poor child. Upstairs, Thomas, the garden room—there's a balcony for the cat.'

He paused for a second by her. 'Bless you, you've thought of everything.'

He went on up the staircase and she received Brimble in his basket and went up after him at a more leisurely pace.

Sir Thomas laid Mary Jane on the bed and carefully unrolled her out of the quilt and Mrs Beaver tucked the bedclothes around her. 'There, there,' she said comfortably, 'the poor young thing. Just you go away, Sir Thomas, and I'll have her put to rights in no time at all. A nice wash and a clean nightie and some of my lemonade.'

Mrs Latimer, coming into the room, nodded her head, set Brimble's basket down on the covered balcony and put a hand on her son's sleeve. 'Shall I get Dr Finney?'

'I'll have a look at her when you've tidied her up. The sooner I get her on to antibiotics the better. You might get him up tomorrow if you would, Mother.'

'Yes, dear. Now go away and have a drink or something and we'll let you know when we are ready for you.'

When he went upstairs again Mary Jane was awake; save for her eyes there was no colour in her face but her hair had been brushed and hung, neatly plaited, over one shoulder and she was wearing one of Mrs Latimer's nighties.

'That's better.' He came and sat on the edge of the
bed and felt her pulse. It was galloping along at a fine
rate and he frowned a little. 'I'm going to start you
off on an antibiotic,' he told her. He spoke with
pleasant remoteness, a doctor visiting his patient. 'An
injection. I'll get it ready while Mrs Beaver turns you
over.'

She couldn't be bothered to answer him; now that
she was clean and in a warm bed all she wanted to
do was sleep. 'Where's Brimble?' she asked suddenly,
and rolled over obedient to Mrs Beaver's kind hands.

'Having a snack on the balcony,' said Sir Thomas,
sliding in the needle as Mrs Beaver drew back the bedclothes and ignoring Mary Jane's startled yelp.

'There, dearie, all over,' said Mrs Beaver. 'You just
turn over on to the other side and have a little nap.'

'It's sore.' Mary Jane's hoarse voice sounded ag-
grieved; tears weren't far off.

'Here's Brimble,' said Sir Thomas. She heard his
voice, remote and kind and felt Brimble's small furry
body beside her, closed her eyes on threatening tears
and went to sleep.

Sir Thomas stood for a moment looking down at
her. She looked not a day over fifteen . . .

Downstairs he found his mother sitting in the
drawing-room. 'I think I will ring Finney,' he told
her, 'explain the circumstances.'

She agreed, 'Yes, dear. I'll take good care of her—
it is flu?'

'Yes, but I suspect that there's a mild pneumonia
as well. I have no idea how long she was lying there
ill.'

'You would have thought that the neighbours would
have noticed that the tea-room was closed.'

'Normally, yes, but with this bad weather it would seem normal enough for her not to open, don't you think?'

When he came back from phoning they went to a belated lunch and as they drank their coffee Mrs Latimer asked, 'Has she no family at all? Did you not mention a sister? She should be told.'

'Felicity—yes, of course, if she is in London. I gather that she seldom is, but I have her address and phone number.' He saw his mother's look of surprise and smiled a little. 'I'll look her up. I'm free for the rest of today.'

'If you do see her, Thomas, and she is anxious about Mary Jane, do tell her that she is very welcome to come here and make sure that she is all right.'

'Thank you, dear.' They were back in the drawing-room and Mrs Latimer began to talk about other things until presently Sir Thomas said, 'I think I'll just take a quick look at Mary Jane before I go. Is Mrs Beaver in the kitchen or in her own room?'

Mrs Latimer glanced at the clock. 'In the kitchen getting the tea-tray ready.'

He went first to look at Mary Jane, deeply asleep now, one arm flung around Brimble. Her washed out face had a little colour now and her breathing was easier; he took her pulse and put a hand on her forehead and then went downstairs to find Mrs Beaver. 'Wake her and wash her and give her plenty to drink and something to eat if she fancies it—yoghurt or something similar. Dr Finney will come in the morning and give you fresh instructions. Thank you, Mrs Beaver—it will only be for a couple of days; I believe she is through the worst of it.'

He drank his tea, promised his mother that he would phone her that evening and drove back to London, leaving his parent thoughtful.

Mary Jane, unaware of his departure and indeed rather hazy as to whether she had seen him at all, woke to find Mrs Latimer sitting by the bed. She still felt ill and weary but her headache was better and she was warm.

When she tried to sit up Mrs Latimer said, 'No, dear, just lie still. We are going to wash your face and hands and make you comfortable and then you are going to eat a little something. Thomas told me to be sure that you did and presently he will telephone to find out if I have done as he asked.'

She smiled so kindly that Mary Jane, to her shame, felt tears fill her eyes and spill down her cheeks. Mrs Latimer said nothing, merely wiped them away and told her that she was getting better and then Mrs Beaver came in with a basin and towels and Brimble was coaxed away to eat his supper on the balcony while she was washed and her hair combed. She lay passive while the two ladies tidied her, fighting a fresh desire to burst into tears; she had looked after herself for so long that she had forgotten how marvellous it was to be cosseted with such care and gentleness.

Mrs Latimer saw the tears. 'Cry if you want to, my dear. I'm sure you're not a watering pot normally, it's just the flu. You're going to feel so much better in the morning.'

She was quite right. Mary Jane woke feeling as though she had been put through a mangle, but her head was clear; she even wished to get up, to be sternly discouraged by Mrs Beaver, standing over her while she drank her tea and ate some scrambled egg.

'If you would tell me,' began Mary Jane.

'All in good time, miss, you just lie there and get well—bless you, a day or two in bed'll do you all the good in the world and you could do with a bit of flesh on those bones.'

Sir Thomas telephoned as his mother was sitting down to breakfast; he had phoned on the previous evening to tell her that he had rung Felicity and was taking her out to dinner later; now he wanted to know how Mary Jane was and Mrs Latimer said carefully, 'Well, Thomas, I don't know much about it, but she seems better. Very limp and still rather hot but she's had several cups of tea and a few mouthfuls of scrambled egg. I gave her the pills you left for her to take. What did her sister say?'

He didn't answer at once. Felicity had been charming when he had phoned, expressed concern about Mary Jane and begged him to go and see her at her flat. He hadn't wanted to do that; instead he had arranged to take her out to dinner and over that meal he had told her about Mary Jane. She had listened for a few minutes and then smiled charmingly at him across the table. 'She'll be all right, she's awfully tough—it's very kind of you to bother.' She had put out a hand and touched his on the table. 'Could we go somewhere and dance?'

He had refused with beautiful manners, pleading patients to see and the hospital to visit and had driven her back to her flat, and when she had asked him where he lived he had evaded her question.

'She told me that Mary Jane would be all right, that she was tough—oh, and that it was kind of us to bother.'

'I see,' said Mrs Latimer, who didn't. 'Dr Finney will be here presently, will you be at your rooms? He could phone you there.'

'Yes, ask him to do that, will you? I'll phone you this evening— I don't think I'll have time before then.'

He rang off and Mrs Latimer finished her breakfast and went back to Mary Jane. 'My doctor is coming to see you presently; perhaps we can tidy you up first?'

'I could get up,' began Mary Jane. 'I feel much better. I'm giving you so much trouble and you are so kind...'

'It's delightful to have someone to fuss over, my dear. Thomas, as you can imagine, has long outgrown any attempts of mine to cosset him. How would you like a nice warm bath before Dr Finney comes and then pop back into bed?'

Mary Jane was sitting up very clean and fresh in another of her hostess's nighties, still pale and limp but doing her best to appear her normal self, when Dr Finney came. He was elderly and rather slow and very kind.

He examined Mary Jane very thoroughly, tapping her chest and thumping her gently and bidding her say 'nine nine nine' and put out her tongue. All these things done, he said thoughtfully, 'A narrow squeak, young lady; another day and you would have been in hospital with pneumonia. Most fortunate that Thomas found you and acted quickly. Another two days in bed and then you may return to your home. You don't have a job?'

'I run a tea-room.'

'Do you, indeed? How interesting. By all means return to it but don't attempt to exert yourself for a few more days. Take the pills which Thomas has left you and there's no reason why you shouldn't get out of bed from time to time and walk round.' His eye lighted on Brimble who had just come in and had jumped on to the bed. 'A cat? Bless my soul!'

'He is mine, Sir Thomas brought him here with me.'

'Of course. I shall come and see you again in two days' time, young lady, and I expect to find you very much better.'

When Mrs Latimer came back presently Mary Jane said, 'I can't think why Sir Thomas brought me here. That sounds awfully rude but you do understand what I mean, Mrs Latimer. I could have gone to...' She paused because she couldn't think of anywhere, only Margaret, who wouldn't have had her anyway, and Miss Kemble who would have had her and nursed her, too, but only because of a strong sense of duty. All her other friends lived in small houses with children or elderly grannies or grandpas in the spare bedrooms.

'I think,' said Mrs Latimer carefully, 'that Thomas realised that by the time he had found someone in the village who could spare the time to look after you you would have been fit only for the hospital and that would have been such an upheaval, wouldn't it, dear?'

'If I had some clothes I could go home as soon as Dr Finney says I may. I don't want to put you to any more trouble, I can never thank you enough.'

'We can talk about that in two days' time; now you are going to have a nap and presently Mrs Beaver will bring you a little lunch. Remember, my dear, that we are really enjoying having you here even though you aren't well. Allow two elderly ladies to spoil you.'

Mrs Latimer smiled at her and went away and Mary Jane closed her eyes and slept, with the faithful Brimble curled up against her.

It was amazing what two days of good food and ample rest did for Mary Jane. Her hair, washed by Mrs Beaver, shone with soft brown lights, her face lost its pinched look and its colour returned and her eyes regained their sparkle. Not pretty, but nice to look at, reflected Mrs Latimer.

After Dr Finney had been to see her again Mary Jane asked diffidently if someone could possibly get her clothes so that she might return home, 'For I have trespassed on your kindness too long,' she pointed out. 'If only I had the key, Mrs Adams could go and get me the clothes and send them at once.'

Mrs Latimer looked vague. 'Well, I suppose that Thomas has the key, my dear, but since he will be coming tomorrow, I'm sure he will know what is best to be done.'

So Mary Jane, wrapped in one of her hostess's quilted dressing-gowns, spent a happy day being shown round the house and sitting in Mrs Latimer's pretty little sitting-room at the back of the hall, listening to that lady talking about Thomas. She longed to ask why, at the age of thirty-four, he wasn't married. Perhaps he was divorced or loved someone already married to another man, perhaps she had died young... Mary Jane, with a lively imagination, allowed it to run riot.

He arrived the next day after lunch and he wasn't alone. Felicity got out of the car and accompanied him into the house, was introduced to his mother and made a pretty little speech to her; she had found that she had a couple of days free and on the spur of the moment she had telephoned to Sir Thomas and asked if she might accompany him if and when he next went to his home. 'I have been anxious about Mary Jane,' she added with one of her charming smiles. Mrs Latimer hid her doubts about that, welcomed her warmly and suggested that she might like to go and see Mary Jane at once.

'Oh, yes, please. She isn't infectious, is she? I have several bookings next week; I have to be careful...'

Mrs Latimer led her upstairs, leaving Sir Thomas to go into the drawing-room with Watson where presently she joined him.

'What a very pretty girl,' she observed, sitting down by the fire. Her voice was dry and he looked at her, smiling a little.

'Beautiful. I'm sorry not to have let you know, but I had no time, I was on the point of leaving when she phoned. I could do nothing else but suggest that she could come.'

'Of course, dear. She expects to stay the night, I dare say.'

'She has an overnight bag with her—said something about putting up at the local pub.'

'No, no, she must stay here. I dare say Mary Jane is delighted to see her.' She didn't look at her son. 'The dear child is so anxious to go back to her tearoom but of course she has no clothes. What do you suggest?'

'I'll drive over presently, take Mrs Beaver with me and fetch what she needs. The place was in a mess; perhaps we could tidy it up a little before I take her back.'

'Do you suppose her sister will go with her and stay a day or two?'

'Unlikely...' He broke off as Felicity came into the room.

'May I come in? Mary Jane is resting so I didn't stay long. What a lovely house you have, Mrs Latimer. I do love old houses; I'd love to see round it.'

She sat down near Sir Thomas and smiled enchantingly at him, and he wondered how two sisters could be so unlike each other. 'I'll go and take a look at her,' he said blandly, 'see if she's fit to go home.'

'I'll come with you,' said Felicity.

'No, no. If she is resting, the fewer visitors she has, the better.'

He took no notice of her pretty little *moue* of disappointment and went away. First to the kitchen to see Mrs Beaver and then upstairs, where he found Mary Jane not resting at all but sitting in a chair with Brimble on her knee, looking out of the window at the dull weather outside.

'Not resting?' he asked, and pulled up a chair to sit beside her. 'Felicity said that you were. How are you?'

'I'm quite well, thank you, Sir Thomas. It was very kind of you to invite Felicity.'

He didn't answer that but observed, 'I hear that you would like to get back to your cottage. I'm going to take Mrs Beaver over there now. Make a list of what you need and we'll bring your things back and I'll drive you over first thing tomorrow morning.'

'I could go as soon as you come back...'

'And so you could, but you're not going to. Another night here won't do you any harm and my mother is loath to let you go.' He got out his pocket-book and a pen and handed them to her. 'Make your list. Mrs Beaver is waiting.'

He was brisk and businesslike so she did her best to be the same, making a careful list with directions as to where everything was. Handing it to him, she tried once more. 'I could go back this afternoon if you wouldn't mind taking me, really I could.'

'Don't be obstinate,' said Sir Thomas, and went away to come back within a few minutes with Mrs Beaver, hatted and coated in case Mary Jane had forgotten something. 'There's no reason why you shouldn't come downstairs and have tea with my mother and Felicity,' he said kindly, and pulled her gently out of her chair. 'Bring Brimble; it's time he and Watson met.'

So she went downstairs and met Watson waiting patiently at the bottom of the stairs for his master. He sniffed delicately at Brimble and Brimble eyed him from the shelter of Mary Jane's arms and muttered before they went into the drawing-room.

'Mary Jane's coming down for tea—we'll be back in good time for dinner.'

'You're not taking Mary Jane back?' Felicity sounded flurried. 'She hasn't any clothes here?'

'We're going to fetch them now.'

'Oh, then I'll come with you...' Felicity had jumped up.

'Mrs Beaver is coming, she knows what to get, but it's good of you to offer.'

He whistled to Watson and went away, leaving the three of them to chat over their tea. At least Felicity did most of the talking, relating titbits of gossip about the people she had met, the glamorous clothes she modelled and the delightful life she led. 'Of course,' she told Mrs Latimer airily, 'I shall give it all up when I marry but it will be so useful—I mean, knowing about clothes and make-up and being social.'

'You are engaged?' asked Mrs Latimer.

'No, not yet. I've had ever so many chances but I know the kind of man I intend to marry—plenty of money, because I'm used to that, a good social background, good looks.' She gave a little tinkling laugh. 'I'll make a good wife to a man with a successful career.'

All the while she talked Mary Jane sat quietly. Sir Thomas, she reflected, was exactly the kind of husband her sister intended to marry, and she was pretty and amusing enough for him to fall in love with her—and he had invited her to come to his mother's home, hadn't he? He had not answered her but he hadn't denied it either. Mrs Latimer quietly took the conversation into her own hands presently and suggested taking Felicity to her room so that she might tidy herself. 'We dine at eight o'clock,' she told her. 'I do hope you will be comfortable; if there is anything you need, do please ask.'

Mary Jane, left alone with Brimble, began making resolute plans for her return. There would be the baking to see to and the place to clean up, for as far as she could remember it had been in something of a pickle when Sir Thomas had fetched her away. He had been so kind and she had put him to a great deal of trouble, she hoped that Mrs Beaver had been able to find everything easily so that he hadn't had to wait too long. The cottage would be cold; she should have asked him to light the gas fire in the sitting-room and sit there...

He hadn't even been into the sitting-room. He and Mrs Beaver had gone into the cold tea-room and through to the kitchen which was indeed in a pickle.

'You go upstairs and get the clothes,' he told Mrs Beaver. 'I'll tidy up here.'

He had taken off his coat and his jacket and rolled up his shirt-sleeves and boiled several kettles of water, washed everything he could see that needed it, dried them and put them away, found a broom and swept the floor and looked in the cupboard. There was tea there, and sugar and a packet of biscuits, cat food and some porridge oats. The fridge held butter and lard, some rather hard cheese and a few rashers of bacon. He went to the foot of the stairs and called up to Mrs Beaver who was trotting to and fro and she peered down at him from the tiny landing. Before he could speak she observed, 'It's a shocking shame, Sir Thomas, that dear child—two of everything, beautifully washed and ironed and mended to death and a cupboard with almost nothing to wear in it. Good stuff, mind you, but dear knows when she went shopping last.' She drew a breath. 'And that sister of hers in them silks and satins—blood's thicker than water, I say and I don't care who hears me say it.'

'Perhaps something can be done about that. I'm going over to the village shop—it should be open still, there's almost no food in the house. Surely the milkman calls...'

'Look outside the back door, sir...'

The milk was there; he fetched it in and put it in the fridge, got into his coat and walked to the shop where he bought what he hoped were the right groceries and bore them back to stack them in the cupboard.

Mrs Beaver was ready by then; they got back into the car and he half listened to Mrs Beaver's indignant but respectful remarks about young girls being left to fend for themselves. She paused for breath at last and added apologetically, 'I do hope I've not put you out, sir, letting me tongue run away with me like that and you likely as not sweet on the young lady. I must own she's pretty enough to catch any gentleman's eye.'

Sir Thomas agreed placidly.

He found his mother and Mary Jane in the drawing-room, bent over a complicated piece of tapestry. They looked up as he went in and Mary Jane got to her feet. 'I'll go and dress,' she said. 'And thank you very much indeed, Sir Thomas.'

He smiled. 'You look very nice as you are, but I dare say you will feel more yourself in a dress.' He held the door for her as she went into the hall. 'Mrs Beaver's taken your case upstairs. Would you like to leave Brimble here? Watson won't hurt him.'

He took the cat from her and watched her go up the staircase before going back into the room.

'Where is our guest?' he asked.

'She went upstairs to tidy herself. Is the cottage all right for Mary Jane to go back?'

'As clean and tidy as we could make it. I fetched some food from the shop—the lady who owns it said they were beginning to wonder where Mary Jane had gone—no one had been out much because of the bad weather and those that had had supposed that she had closed the tea-room since there was no chance of customers. Her neighbours had been away and the Misses Potter, who call regularly, had been indoors with bad colds. A series of unfortunate events.' He sat down opposite her. 'I'm sure that once she is back the village will rally round—she is very well-liked.'

'I'm not surprised...' Mrs Latimer broke off as the door opened and Felicity came into the room. She had changed into a silk sheath of vivid green, its brevity allowing an excellent view of her shapely legs, its neckline, from Mrs Latimer's point of view, immodest. She walked slowly to join them, giving Sir Thomas time to study her charming if unsuitable appearance. It was a pity that he got to his feet almost without a glance and went to get her a drink.

Ten minutes later Mary Jane joined them, wearing the skirt of her suit and a Marks and Spencer blouse, and this time Sir Thomas allowed his gaze to dwell upon her prosaic person. What he thought was nobody's business; all he said was, 'Ah, Mary Jane, come and sit down and have a glass of sherry.'

CHAPTER FIVE

Mrs Latimer spoke. 'Come and sit by me, Mary Jane. How nice to see you dressed and well again. You have recovered so quickly, too. I'm glad for your sake but we shall miss you. Once you are settled in I shall drive over and have tea with you again.'

Mary Jane's quiet answer was drowned by Felicity's voice. 'How I wish that I could live away from London—I do love the country and the quiet life. Sometimes I wish that I would never need to travel so much again. How I envy you, Mary Jane.'

Not easily aroused to bad temper, Mary Jane found these sentiments too hard to swallow. 'Well, I don't suppose it would matter much if you gave up your modelling—there must be dozens of girls ... I could do with some help, especially in the summer.' She spoke in a matter-of-fact voice, smiling a little. No one would have known that she was seething; first her dull, sensible clothes, highlighted pitilessly by Felicity's *couture* and now this nonsense about wanting to live in the country. Why, she had run away from it just as soon as she could ... Sir Thomas, watching her quiet face from under his eyelids, had a shrewd idea of her thoughts. The contrast between her and her sister was too striking to overlook, especially the clothes; on the other hand, he conceded, Felicity hadn't beautiful eyes the colour of violets.

He said smoothly, 'You would probably find living

in the country very dull, Felicity. Are you working at present?'

'Next week—here in London—perhaps we could meet? And then I'm off to New York for the shows. I was there last year and I had a marvellous time. The parties—you have no idea...'

She embarked on a colourful account of her visit and the three of them listened, Mary Jane with understandable wistfulness, Mrs Latimer with an apparent interest because she had never been ill-mannered in her life, and Sir Thomas with an inscrutable face which gave away nothing of his true feelings.

During dinner, however, Felicity was forced to curb her chatter; Sir Thomas kept the conversation firmly upon mundane matters, and, after drinking coffee with the ladies, he pleaded telephone calls to make and went away to the library, presumably not noticing Felicity's sulky face.

He returned just as Felicity, bored with her companions, declared herself ready for bed.

'Is eight o'clock too early for you?' asked Sir Thomas of Mary Jane. 'I need to be back in town by lunchtime.'

'That's fine,' said Mary Jane. 'But surely I could catch a bus or something...' She frowned. 'All the trouble...'

Felicity had been listening. 'I'll come with you...'

'It would mean getting up at half-past six,' Sir Thomas pointed out suavely.

She hesitated. 'Oh, well, perhaps not. It isn't as if Mary Jane needs anyone any more. I'll be waiting here for you when you get back.'

She smiled her most bewitching smile, quite lost on Sir Thomas who had turned away to speak to his mother.

It was one of those mornings in autumn when night was reluctant to give way to morning. It was raining, too. They left exactly at eight o'clock and Mrs Latimer had come down to see them off. She had embraced Mary Jane warmly and promised to see her again shortly, and now they were in the car driving back to the tea-room, she beside Sir Thomas, Brimble in his basket, indignantly silent on the back seat. There seemed no need for conversation; Mary Jane sensed that her companion had no wish to listen to chatter, not that she was much good at that and at that time of day small talk seemed out of place. However, although for the most part they were silent, it wasn't uneasy. She sat quietly, planning her week while Sir Thomas thought his own thoughts. Presumably they were amusing, for once or twice he smiled.

At the tea-room he took no notice of her protests that she was quite able to be left at its door. He got out, opened the door, reached into the car for Brimble's basket, took her key from her and ushered her into her home.

It was chilly and unwelcoming. 'Wait here,' he told her and went upstairs to light the gas fire, switch on the kitchen light and set Brimble's basket down on the table. He fetched her case then, took it upstairs and found her in the kitchen. 'How very clean and tidy it is,' she told him. 'I'm sure I left it in a frightful mess. Will you have a cup of coffee before you go?'

'I wish I could but I must get back.' He took her hand in his, smiling down at her very kindly. 'Take care of yourself, Mary Jane.'

She stared at him. 'You've been very kind, I can never thank you or Mrs Latimer enough, and thank you for bringing me back.' She offered a hand and he took it, bending to kiss her cheek as he did so. She watched him drive away, wondering if she would ever see him again. Probably not. On the other hand, if he should fall in love with Felicity, she would.

She went into the kitchen and released Brimble, made herself a pot of tea, unpacked her few things and put on her pinny. Customers were unlikely. On the other hand, she had to be ready for them if they did come. She went to turn the sign to 'Open' and only then saw the box on the table by the door. There was a bunch of flowers on it, too—chrysanthemums, the small ones which lasted for weeks, just what was needed to cheer up the tea-room...
She took the lid off the box then, and discovered a cooked chicken, straw potatoes and salad in a covered container, egg custard in a pottery dish and a crock of Stilton cheese; there was even a small bottle of wine.

Much cheered, she arranged the flowers on the tables, got the coffee going and got out her pastry board. As soon as she had made some scones she would sit down and write to Mrs Latimer—Mrs Beaver too—and thank them for their kindness.

There was no sign of Felicity by the time Sir Thomas reached his mother's house. He went to bid his mother goodbye and went in search of Mrs Beaver. He found her in the kitchen. 'Ask Rosie or Tracey——' the girls who came from the village each day to help in the

house '—to go to Miss Seymour's room and tell her
that I am leaving in five minutes. If she is unable to
be ready by then, Mrs Latimer will get a taxi for her
so that she can get to Banbury and get a train to town.'

Felicity was in the hall with a minute to spare and
very put out. 'My make-up,' she moaned prettily, 'I
haven't had time, and I've thrown my things into my
case...' She pouted prettily at Sir Thomas who
remained impervious. 'Perhaps we could stop on the
way...'

He had beautiful manners. 'I'm so sorry, but there
won't be time—I must be at the hospital. Shall we
go?'

She bade Mrs Latimer goodbye with the hope that
she would see her again. 'For I haven't had time to
see your lovely home, have I?' But Mrs Beaver she
ignored, sweeping past her to get into the car.

'You'd never know that they were sisters,' declared
Mrs Beaver sourly. A thought echoed by Sir Thomas
as he swept the Rolls out of the gate and through the
village.

Felicity, accustomed to the admiration of the men
she met, worked hard to attract Sir Thomas, but
although he was a charming companion he remained
aloof, and when he stopped the car outside her flat
she had the feeling that she had made no impression
on him whatsoever. It was a galling thought and a
spur to her determination to get him interested in her.
Obviously, he had no interest in her success as a model
or the glamorous life she led. She would have to
change her tactics. She bade him goodbye in a serious
voice, with no suggestion that they might meet again
and added a rider to the effect that she hoped Mary
Jane would be all right. 'I shall take the first oppor-

tunity to go down and see her,' she assured him, and
he murmured suitably, thinking that the likelihood of
that seemed remote. One could never tell, however;
beneath that frivolous manner there might be a heart
of gold. He thought it unlikely, but he was a tolerant
man, ready to think the best of everything and
everyone. He dismissed her from his mind and drove
to the hospital.

Mary Jane was taking the first batch of scones out
of the oven when her first customers came in. A young
couple barely on speaking terms, the girl having
misread the map and directed her companion in entirely the wrong direction. They sat eyeing each other
stormily over the little vase of flowers. Mary Jane
brought the coffee and they wanted to know just where
they were. She told them and the man muttered,
'We're miles out of our way thanks to my map-reader
here.' He glared at the girl.

'No, you're not,' said Mary Jane. 'Just keep on
this road and turn right at the first crossroads—you're
only a few miles in the wrong direction.'

She left them to their coffee and presently the door
opened and the Misses Potter came in.

'Not our usual time, my dear,' said Miss Emily,
'but we were on our way to the stores and saw that
you were back. Have you had a nice little break?'

Mary Jane said that, yes, she had and fetched the
coffee pot just as Miss Kemble came in. 'I see you're
back,' she said briskly. 'You have enjoyed your
holiday, Mary Jane?'

It didn't seem worthwhile explaining. Mary Jane
said that yes, she had, and poured more coffee. The
young couple went presently, on speaking terms once

more, and a tall, thin man with a drooping moustache came in and asked for lunch.

She hadn't had time to make sausage rolls and the demand for lunch during the winter was so small that she could only offer soup and sandwiches. She went to the kitchen to open the soup and slice bread, reflecting as she did so that someone had stocked up the fridge while she had been away. She would have to ask Mrs Latimer...

By one o'clock everyone had gone; she made herself some coffee, ate biscuits and cheese, fed Brimble and went upstairs. Beyond a quick look round she had had no time to put anything away and the bed would have to be made up.

That had been done and very neatly too, and so, when she looked, had her nightie been washed and ironed and folded away tidily. The bathroom was spotless and there wasn't a speck of dust anywhere. It was like having a fairy godmother.

She got into her outdoor things and went to the stores, exchanged the time of day with its owner and asked to use the phone. Mrs Latimer sounded pleased to hear from her and Mary Jane thanked her again for her kindness and then asked, 'Someone cleaned the cottage for me and the fridge is full of food and everything is washed and ironed. Did Sir Thomas...no sorry, I'm being silly, I'm sure he's never ironed anything in his life or bought groceries.'

Mrs Latimer chuckled. 'He certainly brought the food and I'm sure if he had to iron he would, and very well too. No, my dear, he took Mrs Beaver with him, she sorted out your things and together they tidied your cottage. Thomas is a dab hand at washing up.'

'Is he really?' said Mary Jane, much astonished. 'If I write him a note could you please send it on to him? And will you thank Mrs Beaver? As soon as I have time I'll write to you and her as well.'

'We look forward to that, my dear. Have you opened your tea-room yet?'

'Yes, and had customers too. I'm going back now to open until five o'clock although I don't expect anyone will come.'

They wished each other goodbye and she rang off and hurried back to her cottage. No one came that afternoon; she locked the door and went to get her supper, carrying the delicacies upstairs to the sitting-room to eat by the gas fire, with Brimble, on the lookout for morsels of chicken, sitting as close as he could get.

Her supper finished, she sat down to write her letters. Those to Mrs Latimer and Mrs Beaver were quickly done, but the note to Sir Thomas needed both time and thought. He had been kind and very helpful but not exactly friendly; it was hard to strike the right note and it took several wasted sheets of paper before she was satisfied with the result. By then it was time to go to bed.

She saw few customers during the following days. Doing her careful sums each evening, she decided that she was barely paying her way; there was certainly nothing to spare once her modest bills were paid. The winter always was a thin time, of course; it was just a question of hanging on until the spring. Looking out of the window at the dull autumn day, the spring looked a long way off. Luckily, there was Christmas; it might not bring more customers but those who came were usually full of the Christmas spirit and inclined to spend more. She was a neat-fingered girl and not easily depressed; in the tiny loft there was an old-fashioned trunk stuffed with old-fashioned clothes which had belonged to her mother. She got on to a chair and poked her head through the narrow opening. The loft was very small and cold and she wriggled into it and heard the scrabble of mouse feet, but mice or no mice she wasn't going to be put off. She leaned in as far as she was able and dragged the trunk over to the opening. She wouldn't be able to get it down into the cottage but she could open it and see if there was anything she could use.

There was. A gauzy scarf, yards of lace, bundles of ribbons, a watered silk petticoat, balls of wool still usable. She dragged them out, closed the trapdoor and examined her finds at her leisure. The wool was fine and in pale colours, splendid for dolls' clothes, even baby clothes, and the lace and ribbons and silk could be turned into the kinds of things people bought at Christmas: pincushions, lavender bags, beribboned nightdress cases—rather useless trifles but people bought them none the less. She went to bed that night, her head full of plans.

There was a card from Felicity in the morning: she was off to New York in two days' time and she had had a meal with Thomas—they would meet again when she got back. She didn't ask how Mary Jane was but Mary Jane hadn't expected that, anyway. She read the card again; she wasn't really surprised that Sir Thomas had been seeing Felicity, but it made her vaguely unhappy. 'And that's silly,' she told Brimble, his whiskered face buried in his breakfast saucer. 'For she's such a very pretty girl and her clothes are lovely. Perhaps she'll come and see us before Christmas,' and

then, because that was what she had really been
thinking about, she added, 'I wonder what meal it
was and where they went?'

Sir Thomas could have told her if he had been there;
he had been waylaid—there was no other word for
it—by Felicity, who had taken pains to find out where
he lived and had just happened to be walking past his
house as he returned from the hospital. That she had
done this three evenings running without success was
something she didn't disclose but she evinced delighted surprise at seeing him again. 'Perhaps we could
have dinner together?' she had suggested. 'You must
need cheering up after a hard day's work.'

Sir Thomas had been tired, he had wanted his
dinner and a peaceful evening with no one but Watson
for company while he caught up with the medical
journals, but his manners were too nice to have said
so; instead he had suggested that they had a drink in
a pleasant little bar not too far away, 'For I have to
go back to the hospital shortly and I have any amount
of work to do this evening.'

She had pouted prettily and agreed and jumped into
the car; she had great faith in her charm and good
looks, and had no doubt that once they sat down she
could persuade him to take her on to dinner—let the
hospital wait, he was an important man and must
surely do what he wanted to do; he wasn't some junior
doctor at everyone's beck and call.

She was, of course, mistaken, and half an hour later
she had found herself being put into a taxi with no
more than a brisk handshake and regrets that he must
cut short an enjoyable meeting. 'I had hoped you
could drive me to my flat,' she had complained

prettily, and turned her lovely face up to his. 'I do
hate going home alone.'

Sir Thomas had handed the cabby some money.
'You must have many friends, Felicity; I'm sure you
won't be alone for long.' He had lifted a hand in casual
salute as the taxi drove off.

Tremble had come fussing into the hall as he opened
the door of his house and Watson had come to meet
him.

'You're late, Sir Thomas—a bad day, perhaps?'

'No, no, Tremble, only the last hour or so. Give
me ten minutes, will you, while I go through the post?'

He had gone into his study with the faithful Watson
and leafed through his letters without paying much
attention to them. He had had to waste part of an
evening listening to Felicity's airy chatter, and he had
found her tedious. 'A beautiful girl,' he told Watson.
'There's no denying that, and charming too. Perhaps
I am getting middle-aged . . .'

It was much later that evening, standing by the
French windows leading to the small garden behind
the house, waiting for Watson to come in, that he had
decided that he would drive down to see how Mary
Jane was getting on. Her stiff little note of thanks had
amused him, it had so obviously taken time and
thought to compose, but she had given no hint as to
how she was. It would, he told himself, be only civil
to go and see her and make sure that she was quite
well again. He was free on Sunday . . .

Customers had been thin on the ground that week;
the Misses Potter came, as usual, of course, and one
or two women from the village on their way home
from shopping and the very occasional car. Mary Jane

told herself that things would improve and started on her needlework. She had neat, clever fingers and a splendid imagination; in no time at all she had a row of mice, fashioned from the petticoat and wearing lace caps on their tiny heads and frilly beribboned skirts. Quite useless but pretty trifles that she hoped someone would buy. She was rather uncertain what she should ask for them and settled on fifty pence, which Miss Emily Potter told her was far too low a price. All the same she bought one and told Miss Kemble about them. That lady bought one too, declaring it was just the thing for a birthday present for her niece. Mary Jane thought it rather a poor sort of present but perhaps she didn't like the niece very much. Selling two of the mice so quickly gave her the heart to continue with her sewing. She sat them on the counter so that anyone paying for their coffee would see them and, very much encouraged by a passing motorist buying three of them, began on a series of frivolous heart-shaped pincushions.

When Sir Thomas drew up outside the tea-room she was standing on the counter stowing away the potted fern which was usually on it so that there was more room for the mice. She had left the 'Open' sign on the door in the hope that a customer or two might come and she turned round as the door was opened and the bell rang.

Sir Thomas's bulk, elegantly clothed in cashmere, filled the doorway. His, 'Good morning, Mary Jane,' was pleasantly casual, which gave her time to change the expression of delight on her face to one of nothing more than polite surprise. But not before Sir Thomas had seen it.

He wasn't a man to mince his words. 'I thought we might have lunch together; may I bring Watson in?'

'Of course bring him in. It's warm in the kitchen. Brimble's there.'

Sir Thomas fetched the dog, shut the door behind him and took off his coat. 'Where would you like to go?' he asked.

'Well, thank you all the same, but I've made a chicken casserole—Mrs Fellowes keeps poultry and she gave me one—already killed, of course. It's in the oven now and I wouldn't like to waste it. It's a French recipe, thyme and parsley and a bay leaf and a small onion. There should be brandy too, but I haven't any so I used the cooking sherry left over from last Christmas.'

Sir Thomas, who had never before had an invitation refused, listened, fascinated. His magnificent nose quivered at the faint aroma coming from the kitchen. With commendable promptness he said, 'Delicious. May I stay to lunch?'

Mary Jane was still standing on the counter. She looked down at him a little uncertainly. 'Well, if you would like to...'

'Indeed I would.' He crossed the room and stretched up and lifted her down, reflecting that she was a little too thin. He saw the mice then and picked one up. 'And what exactly are these bits of nonsense?'

'Well, I'm not very busy at this time of year, so I thought I'd make something to sell—for Christmas you know.'

He studied it and held it in the palm of his hand. 'My mother would love one, and Mrs Beaver. May I have two—how much are they?'

Mary Jane went very pink. 'I would prefer to give them to you, if you don't mind. If you will choose two I will wrap them up.'

He would have to be more careful, Sir Thomas told himself, watching her wrap the mice in tissue paper. Mary Jane was proud-hearted; she might have few possessions but she had the right kind of pride. He asked casually after the Misses Potter, wanted to know if her cousin had been annoying her lately and had her laughing presently over some of Watson's antics.

'Do you mind sitting in the kitchen?' She led the way to where the two animals were sitting amicably enough side by side before the cooking stove. 'I'll make some coffee and put the fire on upstairs.'

'I'll do that,' he said, and when he was downstairs again, he asked, 'Are there any odd jobs to be done while I'm here?'

'Would you reach up and get two plates from that top shelf? I don't often use them but they belonged to my mother.'

He reached up and put them on the table. 'Coalport—the Japan pattern—eighteenth-century? No, early nineteenth, isn't it? Delightful and very valuable, even just two plates.'

'Yes, we always used them when I was a little girl. I never discovered what happened to them all when we came to live with Uncle Matthew. When I came here Cousin Oliver told me that I could take a few plates and cups and saucers with me so I took these. I found them at the back of the china pantry.'

'The casserole will taste twice as good on them. Do you want me to peel potatoes or clean these sprouts?'

She gave him an astonished look. 'But you can't do that. At least, what I mean is you mustn't, you might cut your hands and then you couldn't operate.'

'Then I'll make the coffee ...'

The little kitchen was very crowded, what with Sir Thomas and his massive frame taking up most of it and Watson and Brimble getting under their feet. He made the coffee and carried it up to the sitting-room, closely followed by Watson, Mary Jane and Brimble. He had switched on the little reading lamp and the room looked cosy. Sir Thomas stretched out his long legs and drank his coffee. He thought that Mary Jane was very restful; there was no need to talk just for the sake of talking and she was quite unselfconscious. Presently he suggested, 'Would you like to drive around for a while this afternoon? Even in the winter the Cotswolds are always delightful.'

'That would be nice, but isn't there something else you'd rather do?'

He hid a smile, 'No, Mary Jane, there isn't.'

'Well, then, I'd like that very much.' She put down her mug. 'There's the bell.'

Three elderly ladies nipped with the cold, wanting coffee and biscuits and, when the aroma from the casserole reached them, wanting lunch as well. Sir Thomas could hear Mary Jane apologising in her pretty voice and reflected that if he hadn't been there she would have probably offered to share her dinner with them. As it was, she gave them very careful instructions as to how to get to Stow-on-the-Wold where, she assured them they could get an excellent lunch at the Union Crest.

When they had gone Sir Thomas went downstairs and locked the door and turned the notice to 'Closed'.

'For nothing,' he explained, 'must hinder my enjoyment of the casserole.'

It was certainly delicious; Mary Jane had creamed the potatoes and cooked the sprouts to exactly the right moment, grated nutmeg over them and added a dollop of butter, thus adding to the perfection of the chicken.

Mary Jane had laid the kitchen table with care and, although they drank water from the tap and everything was dished up from the stove, the meal was as elegant as any in a West End restaurant. Mary Jane didn't quite believe him when he said that, but it was nice of him to say so.

They washed up together while Watson and Brimble ate their own hearty meal and, since the days were getting short now and the evenings came all too quickly, Sir Thomas took Watson for a brisk walk while Mary Jane got into her elderly winter coat, made sure that Brimble was cosy in his basket and, being a good housewife, went round turning off everything that needed to be turned off, shut windows and locked the back door securely.

Sir Thomas ushered her into the car, settled Watson on the back seat and went to lock the tea-room door.

'Have you any preference as to where we should go?' he asked her.

Mary Jane, very comfortable in the leather seat and quietly happy at the prospect of his company for an hour or so, had no preference at all.

He turned the car and went out of the village on the Gloucester road to turn off after a mile or so into the country. The road was narrow and there were few villages and almost no traffic. The big car went smoothly between the hedges allowing them views on either side.

'You know this part of the country?' asked Sir Thomas.

'No, not well; I've never been on this road before. It's delightful.'

'It will take us to Broadway. There's another very quiet road from there to Pershore...'

At Pershore he turned south to Tewkesbury where he stopped at the Bell and gave her a splendid tea with Watson under the table, gobbling up the morsels of crumpets and cake which came his way. 'Your scones are much better,' declared Sir Thomas.

She thanked him shyly and took another crumpet.

It was already dusk and, in the car once more, he turned for home, still keeping to the side-roads so that it was almost dark by the time they got back to the tea-room.

When she would have thanked him and got out of the car he put a hand over hers on the door-handle. 'No, wait.' And he took the key and went in to switch on the lights and go upstairs to turn on the fire. Only then did he come back to the car.

They went in together and Mary Jane said, 'I don't suppose you would like a cup of coffee?' And when he shook his head, 'I expect you've got something to do this evening.' She spoke cheerfully, thinking that he must have found her dull company. Perhaps he would have a delightful evening with some beautiful witty girl who would have him laugh. He hadn't laughed much all day, only smiled from time to time...

He stood watching her. Her unexpected outing had given her a pretty colour and her eyes shone. She offered her hand now. 'It was a lovely day—thank you very much. Please remember me to your mother and Mrs Beaver when you see them.' She smiled up at him. 'Did you have a pleasant evening with Felicity? She sent me a card. She's great fun.'

Sir Thomas, versed in the art of concealing his true feelings under a bland face, agreed pleasantly while reflecting that no two sisters could be more unlike each other and why had Felicity made a point of telling Mary Jane that she had spent the evening with him? A gross exaggeration to begin with, and what was the point? To make Mary Jane jealous? That seemed to him to be most unlikely; his friendship with her was of the most prosaic kind, brought about by circumstances.

He got into his car and drove back to London to his quiet house and a long evening in his study, making notes for a lecture he was to give during the coming week. But presently he put his pen down and sat back in his chair. 'You enjoyed your day?' he enquired of Watson, lying half-sleep before the fire. 'Delightful, wasn't it? I think that we must do it again.' He opened his diary. 'Let me see, when do I next go to Cheltenham?'

Watson opened an eye and thumped his tail. 'You agree? Good. Now let me see, whom do we know living not too far from the village?'

Mary Jane watched the tail-lights of the Rolls disappear down the village street and then locked the door and went to feed Brimble. She wasn't very hungry but supper would be something to do. She poached an egg and made some toast and a pot of tea and took the tray upstairs and sat by the gas fire while she ate her small meal. It had been a lovely day but she mustn't allow herself to get too interested in Sir Thomas. The thought occurred to her that perhaps since Felicity wasn't there to be taken out, he had taken the opportunity to see more of her. If he was falling in love with her sister then he would want to be on good terms with herself wouldn't he? She should have talked more about Felicity so that if he had wanted to, he could have talked about her too. For some reason she began to feel unhappy, which was silly since Sir Thomas and Felicity would make a splendid couple. Perhaps she was being a bit premature in supposing that he had fallen in love, but he was bound to if he saw more of her sister; all the men she met fell in love with her sooner or later. Mary Jane was sure of that, for Felicity had told her so.

Autumn had given way to winter without putting up much of a fight and everyone was thinking about Christmas. The village stores stocked up on paper chains for the children to make and a shelf full of sweet biscuits and boxes of sweets. Mary Jane made a cake and iced it and stuck Father Christmas at its centre and put it in her window with two red candles and a 'Merry Christmas' stuck on to the window. Christmas was still a few weeks off, but with the red lampshades she had made the tea-room look welcoming. Surprisingly, for the next day or two she had more customers than she had had for weeks. She sold the mice too, stitching away each evening, replenishing her stock.

She had another card from Felicity. She was back in London to do some modelling for a glossy magazine but she intended to spend Christmas at her flat. There was no point in asking Mary Jane to join her there, she had written, for she knew how much she hated leaving the cottage. She wouldn't have gone, she told herself, even if she had been invited, for she knew none of Felicity's friends and hadn't the right clothes. All the same, it would have been nice to have been asked.

The next day Mrs Latimer came, bringing with her a little dumpling of a woman with a happy face. The Misses Potter were sitting at their usual place but there was no one else there. Mrs Latimer went over to the counter to where Mary Jane was getting out cups and saucers. 'How nice to see you again, my dear, and looking a lot better, too. I've come for tea—some of your nice scones? And come and meet someone who knows about you and your family...

'Mrs Bennett, this is Mary Jane Seymour—Mary Jane, Mrs Bennett was a friend of your mother's.'

The little lady beamed. 'You were a very little girl—you won't remember me, your mother and I lost touch. I heard that you and your sister had gone to live with your uncle and of course Felicity is quite famous, isn't she? However, I had no idea that you were here. I wrote once or twice to your uncle but he never answered. It's lovely to see you again, and with a career too!'

'Well, it's only a tea-room,' said Mary Jane, liking her new customer. 'Do sit down and I'll bring you your tea.'

The Misses Potter, too ladylike to stare, had been listening avidly. Now they had no excuse to stay any longer for the scones were eaten and the teapot drained. They paid their bill, bowed to the two ladies and went home; news of any sort was welcome, and they looked forward to spreading it as soon as possible.

It was long after closing-time when Mrs Latimer and her friend left and the latter by then had wheedled Mary Jane into accepting her invitation to the buffet supper she was giving in ten days' time. It would mean a new dress, but Mary Jane, feeling reckless, had accepted.

That evening Mrs Latimer phoned her son. 'We had tea with Mary Jane—she's coming to Mrs Bennett's party. Tell me, Thomas, how did you discover that she had known Mary Jane's parents?' She paused. 'Or, for that matter, how did you discover Mrs Bennett? A most amiable woman, apparently not in the least surprised to have a visit from a friend of a friend...'

'Easily enough. Felicity mentioned her and I remembered the name—and phoned a few friends around that part of the country. Thank you for your help, my dear.'

Mrs Latimer was frowning as she put down the phone. Thomas was going to a good deal of trouble to liven up Mary Jane's sober life, she hoped it wasn't because he had fallen in love with Felicity. A man in love would go to great lengths to please a girl, and yet, somehow, he wasn't behaving as though he were. He could of course be sorry for Mary Jane. Mrs Latimer smiled suddenly. That young lady wouldn't thank him for that.

CHAPTER SIX

THE problems of a dress kept Mary Jane wakeful for a few nights. She would have to close the tea-room and go to Cheltenham. She couldn't afford to buy a dress; she would have to find the material and make it herself. There wasn't much time for that, especially as she hadn't a sewing-machine. Mrs Stokes had one and so did Mrs Fellowes and now was no time to be shy about asking to borrow from one of them.

Mrs Fellowes agreed to lend hers at once; moreover, when she heard why Mary Jane wanted it, she offered to give her a lift on the following day to Cheltenham.

She found what she wanted: ribbed silk in a soft dove-grey, just right for the pattern she had chosen, a simple dress with a full skirt, a modest neckline and elbow-length sleeves. She bought matching stockings and, in a fit of recklessness, some matching slippers in grey leather. They could be dyed black, she told herself, so they weren't an extravagance.

Customers were few and far between, which was a good thing, for she was able to cut out the dress and sew it. She had a talent for sewing and the dress, when it was finished, would pass muster just as long as it didn't come under the close scrutiny of someone in the world of fashion. She hung it in her bedroom and spent an evening doing her nails and washing her hair, half wishing that she weren't going to the party. Mrs Bennett seemed friendly and sweet but they didn't really know each other; she had said that there would

109

be a lot of people there and Mary Jane wondered if there would be dancing. She loved to dance, but supposing no one wanted to dance with her?

She would be fetched, Mrs Bennett had told her in a letter; friends who lived in Shipton-under-Wychwood would collect her on their way to Bourton-on-the-Hill, where Mrs Bennett lived.

She was ready long before they arrived, wrapped in her elderly winter coat, cold with sudden panic at the idea of meeting a great many strange people. She need not have worried; the estate car which pulled up at her door was crammed with a cheerful family party, quite ready to absorb her into their number, and if they found the winter coat not quite in keeping with the occasion, no one said so. She was made to feel at home and by the time they arrived she had forgotten her sudden fright and went along to the bedroom set aside for their coats, to be further braced by the two girls and their mother admiring her dress. She needed their reassurance, for she could see that, compared with the dresses the other girls were wearing, hers, while quite suitable, was far too modest. Bare shoulders, tiny shoulder straps and bodices which stayed up by some magic of their own seemed to be the norm. She went down the staircase with the others and into the vast drawing-room in Mrs Bennett's house where her hostess was greeting her guests.

Sir Thomas, talking to his host, watched Mary Jane, a sober moth among the butterflies, pause by Mrs Bennett and exchange brief greetings. Her dress, he considered, suited her very well, although he surprised himself by wondering what she would look like in something pink and cut to show rather more of her person. No jewellery either. A pearl choker, he reflected, would look exactly right around her little neck. He listened attentively to his companion's opinion of modern politics, made suitable replies and presently made his way to where Mary Jane, swept along by her new acquaintances, stood with a group of other young people.

She saw him coming towards her and quite forgot to look cool and casual. Her gentle mouth curved into a wide smile and she flushed a little. He took her hand. 'Hello, Mary Jane, I didn't know that you knew the Bennetts.'

She didn't take her hand away. 'I didn't either. Your mother came the other day and brought Mrs Bennett with her. I think she's a friend of a friend and she remembered me when I was a little girl—she knew my mother.'

'What a delightful surprise for you,' said Sir Thomas gravely, not in the least surprised himself. 'Who brought you?'

'Mr and Mrs Elliott—they live at Shipton-under-Wychwood and called for me. They've been very kind...'

'Ah, yes— I've met them. My mother's here—have you seen her yet?'

'No.' She added rather shyly, 'I don't know anyone here.'

'Soon remedied.' He took her arm and made his way round the room, greeting those he knew and introducing her and finally finding his mother.

'There you are, Thomas—and Mary Jane. How pretty you look, my dear, and what a charming dress—I have never seen so many exposed bosoms in all my life and many of them need covering.' She eyed Mary Jane and added, 'Although I don't think your bosom needs to be concealed; you have a pretty figure, my dear.'

Mary Jane, very pink in the cheeks, thanked her faintly and Sir Thomas, standing between them, stifled a laugh. His mother, a gentle soul by nature, could at times be quite outrageous.

'You agree, Thomas?' She smiled up at her son. 'No, probably you don't. Go away and talk to someone; I want a chat with Mary Jane.'

When they were alone she said, 'My dear, I wanted to ask you—where will you be at Christmas? Not alone, I hope?'

'Me? No, Mrs Latimer, Felicity is in London, you know, and I'm going there. I'm looking forward to it.' She told the lie, valiantly glad that Sir Thomas wasn't there to hear her. She was normally a truthful girl but this, she considered, was an occasion when she must bend the truth a little. After all, there was still time for Felicity to invite her...

'I'm glad to hear that. What do you do with your cat?'

Mary Jane was saved from replying by a dashing young man in a coloured waistcoat. 'I say, if I'm not interrupting, shall we dance? They're just starting up. Sir Thomas introduced us just now—Nick Soames? Remember?'

'Run along, dear,' said Mrs Latimer. 'But don't leave without coming to say goodbye, will you?'

So Mary Jane danced. Nick was a good partner and she had always loved dancing and when the dance finished he handed her over to someone called Bill who didn't dance very well but made her laugh a lot. Now and then she saw Sir Thomas, head and shoulders above everyone else, circling the room with a succession of beautifully dressed girls. From the look of them he certainly hadn't agreed with his mother about the over-exposure of bosoms. They're not decent, decided Mary Jane, swanning round the room in the arms of someone called Matt who talked of nothing but horses.

Mrs Bennett had drawn the line at a disco. It was her party, she had pointed out; the young ones could go somewhere and dance their kind of dancing whenever they liked; in her house they would foxtrot and waltz or not dance at all. The band was just striking up a nice old-fashioned waltz when Sir Thomas whisked Mary Jane away from an elderly gentleman who was on the point of asking her to dance with him.

'I was going to dance with that gentleman,' she pointed out tartly.

'Yes, I know, but he's a shocking dancer; your feet would have been black and blue.' He was going round the edge of the big room. 'Are you enjoying yourself?'

'Yes, very much, thank you. I—I was a bit doubtful at first, I mean, I don't know anyone, but Mrs Bennett has been so kind. She's coming to see me one day after Christmas so that we can talk about my mother and father. Uncle Matthew didn't talk to us much, you know; I dare say he didn't like children, although he was a very kind man.'

The music stopped but he didn't let her go and when it started again he went on dancing with her. She was a little flushed now, but her pale brown hair, pinned in its heavy coil, was as neat as when she had arrived and her small person, so demurely clad, was light in his arms.

He waltzed her expertly through an open door and into a small room where a fire was burning and chairs grouped invitingly.

He sat her down by a small table with an inviting display of tasty bits and pieces in little dishes and a bottle of white wine in a cooler. 'Spare me five minutes of your time and tell me how you are.'

'I'm very well thank you, Sir Thomas.' She popped an olive into her mouth—she had had a sketchy lunch and almost no tea and the buffet supper was still an hour or so away.

'Busy?' He poured wine into two glasses. 'I suppose you will be going to Felicity's for Christmas?' His tone was casual though he watched her carefully from under his lids.

'Christmas,' Mary Jane stalled for a time while she thought up a good fib. 'Oh, yes, of course; I always go each year. It's great fun.'

He didn't believe her but nothing in his calm face showed that.

'How do you go?' he wanted to know, still casual.

'Oh, Felicity fetches me,' said Mary Jane, piling fib upon fib. She hadn't looked at him but had busied herself sampling the potato straws. She flashed him a brief smile. 'I expect you go to Mrs Latimer's?'

'Or she comes to stay with me with various other members of the family.'

He handed her a dish of little biscuits and she selected one carefully.

'I'm glad to see you looking so well.' Sir Thomas handed her her glass. 'Let us drink to your continued good health.'

The wine was delicious and very cold. 'And you,' said Mary Jane. 'I hope you have a very happy

Christmas and don't have to work. I don't suppose you do, anyhow.'

'You suppose wrongly. People break arms and legs and fracture their skulls every day of the year, you know.'

'Well, yes, of course they do but surely you're too important...' She stopped because he was smiling.

'Not a bit of it; if I'm needed to operate or be consulted then I'm available.'

'Do you ever go to other countries?'

'Frequently.'

She had polished off the potato straws and most of the olives.

'May I have the supper dance?' asked Sir Thomas.

'Will that be soon? I'm awfully hungry...'

He glanced at his watch. 'Half an hour; that will soon pass if you are dancing.'

They went back to the drawing-room and he handed her over quite cheerfully to the horsey Matt, who danced her briskly round the room and gave her a detailed account of his last point-to-point. It was a relief when the music stopped and she was claimed by a tall young man with a melancholy face who had no idea how to dance but shambled round while he told her, in gruesome detail, about his anatomy classes. He was a medical student in his third year and anxious to impress her. 'I saw you dancing with Sir Thomas—do you know him?'

'We're acquainted.'

'He's great—you've no idea—to see him fit a prosthesis...'

'Yes, he seems well-known,' said Mary Jane quickly, anxious to avoid the details.

'Well-known? He's famous!' He trod on her foot and she hoped that he hadn't laddered her stockings or ruined her shoe. 'There's no one who can hold a candle to him. I watched him do a spinal graft last week ...' He embarked on the details—every single drop of blood and splinter of bone. Sir Thomas, guiding his hostess round the floor, saw Mary Jane's face and grinned to himself.

The supper dance came next and he went to find her, still listening politely to her companion's description of the instruments needed for the grisly business. Sir Thomas put a large hand on her arm and nodded affably at the young man. 'Our dance, Mary Jane?' he said and led her away.

'It seems you're quite famous,' she observed, her small nose buried in his white shirt-front. 'You never talk about it.'

He said, seriously, 'I don't think I've ever met anyone who would want to hear.'

'How dreadful for you, having to keep it all to yourself.'

'Indeed it is at times but most of my companions wouldn't wish to hear about anything to do with hospitals or patients.'

'No? Well, I wouldn't mind. I'm sure it couldn't be worse than that boy's description of a meni—mensis ...'

'Meniscectomy—the removal of the cartilage of the knee. An operation performed with considerable success and not in the least dramatic.'

He smiled down at her. 'Next time I feel the urge to unburden myself I shall come and see you, Mary Jane.'

She didn't think that he was serious but she said cheerfully, 'You do—I'm not in the least squeamish.'

They went in to supper then, sharing a table with at least half a dozen other guests, eating lobster patties, tiny sausages, cheesey morsels and little squares of toast spread with pâtés and dainty trifles which left Mary Jane feeling hungry still. She drank two glasses of wine, though, and her eyes became an even deeper violet. She would have accepted a third glass of wine if Sir Thomas hadn't pulled her gently to her feet.

'A little exercise?' he suggested suavely, and danced her round the room in a leisurely manner, and when the music stopped took her to where his mother was sitting talking to Mrs Bennett.

'There you are, my dears.' Mrs Latimer beamed at them both. 'Thomas, go away and dance with some of the lovely girls here, I want to talk to Mary Jane.' She realised what she had said, and added, 'I put that very badly, didn't I? Mary Jane is lovely, too.'

Mary Jane smiled a little and sat down and didn't watch Sir Thomas as he went away. It was kind of Mrs Latimer to call her lovely, although it was quite untrue. It would have been nice if Sir Thomas had told her that but of course he never would; she had no illusions as to her mediocre face.

Presently, she was whisked away to dance once more—never mind her lack of looks, she danced well and the men had been quick to see that. She didn't lack partners and she was still full of energy when someone announced the last waltz and she found Sir Thomas beside her.

'I'll take you back,' he told her. 'Will you explain to the people who brought you?'

'Won't they mind?'

'I don't suppose so.' He was holding her very correctly, looking over her head with the air of a man who wasn't very interested in what he was doing. Most of the other couples were dancing very close together in a very romantic fashion but of course, she told herself, there was nothing about her to inspire romance. Perhaps he was wishing it was Felicity in his arms. He'd be holding her a lot tighter...!

She thanked him as the dance ended and after a few minutes of goodbyes went off to fetch her coat. It stood out like a sore thumb among the elegant shawls and cloaks in the hall and she wondered if he was ashamed of her and dismissed the thought as unworthy of him. His place was so sure in society that he had no need to worry about such things.

Mrs Latimer kissed her goodbye. 'We must see you again soon, Mary Jane,' a wish echoed by Mrs Bennett. 'We shall all be busy with Christmas,' she added, 'but in the New Year you must come and spend the day.'

Mary Jane thanked them both and got into the car and sat quietly as Sir Thomas drove away.

Clear of the village, he slowed the car. 'A pleasant evening,' he observed. 'Do you go to many parties at this time of year?'

She couldn't remember when she had last attended a party—the church social evening, of course, and the Misses Potters' evening—parsnip wine and ginger nuts—but they were hardly parties.

'No.' She sought for some light-hearted remark to make and couldn't think of any.

He didn't seem to notice her reticence but began to talk about their evening, a casual rambling talk which needed very little reply.

It was profoundly dark when he drew up before her cottage. He said, 'Stay where you are, and give me the key,' and went and opened the door before coming back for her. At the door he said, 'Hot buttered toast and tea would be nice...'

She turned a startled face to his. 'It's half-past two in the morning.' She smiled suddenly. 'Come in, you can make the toast while I put the kettle on.'

They had it in the kitchen, with Brimble, refreshed by a sleep, sitting between them.

'You don't have to go back to London, do you?' asked Mary Jane.

'No, I'm spending the rest of the night at my mother's. I must be back in town by Monday morning, though. And you?'

'Me? Oh, I'm not doing anything. The tea-room will be open, of course, but there won't be many customers.'

'That will give you time to get ready for your trip to London,' he observed smoothly.

She agreed rather too quickly.

He bade her goodnight presently, bending to kiss her cheek with a casual friendliness. 'I dare say we shall see each other again,' and when she looked puzzled, 'At Felicity's.'

She wished then that she could tell him that she would not be there, that she had allowed him to suppose that she would be with her sister, but somehow she couldn't think of the right words. He had gone before she had conjured up another fib.

She had rather more customers than she had hoped for in the last weeks before Christmas and the mice sold well; she began to cherish the hope that she might go to the January sales and look for a coat. The Misses Potter had invited her for Christmas dinner as they had done for several years now and the church bazaar gave her the opportunity to bake some little cakes for Miss Kemble's stall. And on Christmas Eve the postman handed in a big cardboard box from Harrods. It contained caviar, a variety of pâtés, a tin of ham, a small Christmas pudding and a box of crackers, chocolates and a half-bottle of claret. The slip of paper with it contained a message from Felicity; she knew that Mary Jane would have a lovely Christmas, she herself was up to her ears in parties and there was a wonderful modelling job waiting for her in Switzerland in the New Year. There was a PS 'Saw Thomas yesterday'.

Which was to be expected, reflected Mary Jane, shaking off a sudden sadness.

She went to church at midnight on Christmas Eve and lingered afterwards exchanging greetings with everyone there and then went back to the cottage to drink hot cocoa and go to bed with Brimble heavy on her feet. She wasn't sorry for herself, she told herself stoutly; several people had given her small gifts and she was going to spend the day with the Misses Potter. She wondered what Sir Thomas was doing, probably with Felicity... She fell into a troubled sleep which would have been less troubled had she known that he was bent over the operating table, carefully pinning and plating the legs of a young man who had, under the influence of the Christmas spirit, jumped out of a window on to a concrete pavement.

She took the wine, the crackers and the chocolates with her when she went to the Misses Potter. Brimble she had left snug in his basket, a saucer of his favourite food beside him. Her elderly friends liked her to stay for tea and by the time she had washed the delicate china they used on special occasions, it would be evening. She had put a little Christmas tree in the cottage window and switched on the lights before she left; it would be welcoming when she went home.

Miss Emily had roasted a capon and Miss Mabel had set the table in the small dining-room with a lace-edged cloth, the remnants of the family silver and china and wine glasses and had lighted a branched candlestick. Mary Jane wished them a happy Christmas, kissed their elderly cheeks and handed over the wine.

'Crackers,' declared Miss Emily. 'How delightful, my dear, and chocolates—Bendick's—the very best, too. Let us have a small glass of sherry before lunch.'

It had been a very pleasant day, thought Mary Jane, letting herself into the cottage. Tomorrow she would go for a good walk in the morning and then have a lazy afternoon reading by the fire.

It was raining in the morning and not a soul stirred in the village street. 'It'll be better out than in,' she told Brimble and got into her wellies, her elderly raincoat and tied a scarf over her hair, crammed her hands into woolly gloves and then set out. She took the country road to Icomb, past the old fort, on to Wick Rissington and then she turned for home, very wet and, despite her brisk walking, rather cold.

It was a relief to reach the path at the side of the church, a short cut which would bring her into the main street, opposite the tea-room. She nipped down it smartly and came to a sudden halt. The Rolls was standing before her door and Sir Thomas, apparently impervious to the wind and rain, was leaning against its bonnet, the faithful Watson beside him.

His, 'Good afternoon Mary Jane,' was austere and she had the suspicion that he was concealing ill-humour behind his bland face. It was just bad luck that he should turn up; she was, after all, supposed to be in London, enjoying the high life with Felicity.

She stood in front of him, feeling at a disadvantage; she was wet and bedraggled and the sodden scarf did nothing for her looks.

'Hello, Sir Thomas—how unexpected...'

He took the key from her and opened the door and stood aside to let her enter before following her in. Watson shook himself thankfully and went straight through to the kitchen and Sir Thomas, without asking, took off his coat.

'I expect you'd like a cup of tea,' said Mary Jane, wringing out her headscarf over the sink and kicking off her wellies.

'I expect I would.' He took her raincoat from her and hung it on the hook behind the back door and she went to put on the kettle. It was a little unnerving, she reflected, being confronted like this; she would have to think something up.

She wasn't given the time. 'Well,' said Sir Thomas, 'perhaps you will explain.'

'Explain what?' She busied herself with cups and saucers, wondering if a few more fibs would help the situation. Apparently not.

'Why you are here alone when you should be with Felicity in London.'

'Well...' She spooned tea into the pot and couldn't think of anything to say.

'You told me that you were staying with your sister, and yet I find you here.'

'Yes, well,' began Mary Jane and was halted by his impatient,

'For heaven's sake stop saying "Yes, well"—forget the nonsense and tell me the truth for once.'

She banged the teapot on to the table. 'I always tell you the truth...' She caught his cold stare. 'Well, almost always...'

She sat down opposite him and poured out their tea, handed him a plate of scones and offered Watson a biscuit as Brimble jumped on to her lap.

She decided to take the war into the enemies' camp. 'Why aren't you in London?'

His stern mouth twitched. 'I spent most of Christmas Day with my mother and I'm on my way back to town.'

'You're going the wrong way.'

'Don't be pert. I am well aware which way I am travelling. And now, Mary Jane, since you are unable to string two sentences together, perhaps you will answer my questions.'

'I don't see why I should...'

He ignored this. 'Did Felicity invite you to go to London for Christmas?'

'It's none of your business.' She gave him a defiant look and saw that he had become Sir Thomas Latimer, calm and impersonal and quite sure that he would be answered when he asked a question. She said in a small voice, 'Well, no.' She added idiotically, 'I expect she forgot—you know, she has so many friends and she leads a busy life.'

'Did you not hear from her at all?'

'Oh, yes. She sent me a hamper from Harrods. I don't expect that I would like to go to London anyway, I haven't the right clothes and her friends are awfully clever and witty and I'm not.'

'So why did you lie to me?'

'Well...'

'If you say well just once more, I shall shake you,' he observed pleasantly. 'Tell me, have you ever been to stay with Felicity?'

'W... Actually, no.'

'So why did you lie to me?'

'They were fibs,' she told him sharply. 'Lies hurt people but fibs are useful when you don't want—to interfere or make people feel that they have to help you if you're getting in the way.' She added anxiously, 'Have I made that clear?'

'Oh, yes, in a muddled way. Tell me, Mary Jane, why should you not wish me to know that you would be staying here on your own for Christmas?'

'I have just told you.'

'You think that I have fallen in love with Felicity?'

She looked at him then. 'Everyone falls in love with her, she's so beautiful and she is fun to be with and so successful. Whenever she sends me a card she mentions you so you must know her quite well by now. So you must... yes, I think you must love her.'

She wasn't sure if she liked his smile. 'Would you like me for a brother-in-law, Mary Jane?'

She wondered about the smile; she wouldn't like him for a brother-in-law; she would like him for a husband, and why should she suddenly discover that now of all times, sitting opposite him, being cross-examined as though she were in a witness-box and

fighting a great wish to nip round the table and fling
her arms round his neck and tell him that she loved
him? She would have to say something, for he was
watching her.

'Yes, oh, yes, that would be delightful.' She bent
to pat Watson so that he shouldn't see her face and
was surprised and relieved when Sir Thomas got up.

'Well, I must be off.' He added smoothly, 'Shall I
give your love to Felicity when I see her?'

'Yes, please.' She went to the door with him and
she held out her hand. 'Drive carefully,' she told him.
'Goodbye, Sir Thomas.'

His hand on the door, he paused. 'There is something you should know. Falling in love and loving are
two quite different things. Goodbye.'

He drove away, Watson sitting beside him, and she
went back to the kitchen and began to tidy up. She
told herself that it was extremely silly to cry for no
reason at all, but she went on weeping and Brimble,
wanting his supper and jumping on to her lap to
remind her of that, got a shockingly damp coat.

Presently she dried her eyes. 'Well—no, I mustn't
say well; what I mean to say is I shall forget this
afternoon and take care not to see Sir Thomas again
unless I simply must.'

Brimble, drying his fur, agreed.

It was difficult, though, the tea-shop was open, but
for several days no one came to drink the coffee or
eat the scones she had ready, she filled her days with
odd jobs around the cottage, turning out cupboards
and drawers with tremendous zeal, making plans for
the year ahead; perhaps she should branch out a bit—
do hot lunches? But supposing no one ate them? She

couldn't afford to waste uneaten meals and her freezer
was too small to house more than bare necessities.
Felicity, on one of her flying visits, had suggested,
half laughingly, that she should sell the cottage and
train for something. Mary Jane had asked what and
she had said, carelessly, 'Oh, I don't know—something domestic—children's nurse or something
worthy—a dietician at a hospital or a social worker,
at least you would meet some people. This village is
dead or hadn't you noticed?'

Mary Jane recalled the conversation clearly enough
now and gave it her serious consideration, deciding
that she didn't want to be any of the people Felicity
had suggested and, moreover, that the village wasn't
dead. Quiet, yes, but at least everyone knew everyone
else ...

It was the last day of December when Mrs Bennett
came. She trotted in, her good natured face wreathed
in smiles. 'I'm so glad I found you at home,' she
declared, 'and I do so hope you are not doing anything exciting this evening, for I've come to take you
back with me—to see the New Year in, my dear.'

She sat herself down and Mary Jane sat down on
the other side of the table. 'How very kind of you,
Mrs Bennett, but you see it's a bit difficult—there's
Brimble and I'd have to come home again ...'

Mrs Bennett brushed this aside. 'Put on the coffee-
pot, my dear, and we'll put our heads together.' She
unbuttoned her coat and settled back in her chair.
'Someone will come over for you at about half-past
seven and we'll dine at half-past eight, and I promise
you that directly after midnight someone shall bring
you back here. There won't be many people, just a

few close friends and the family.' She added firmly, 'You can't possibly stay here by yourself, Mary Jane.' She glanced around. 'Your sister isn't here?'

Mary Jane brought the coffee and passed the sugar and milk. 'No, I'm not sure if she is in England—she travels all over the place, you know.'

'So, that settles it,' said Mrs Bennett comfortably. 'Wear that pretty dress you had on at the party, I dare say we shall all be feeling festive, and please don't disappoint me, my dear.'

'I'd love to come, Mrs Bennett, if it's not being too much of a bother collecting me and bringing me back. You're sure the grey dress will do?'

'Quite positive. Now I must be off home and make sure that everything is ready for this evening.'

Mary Jane wasted no time; the contents of a cupboard she had intended to turn out were ruthlessly returned higgledy-piggledy before she set about making her person fit for the evening's entertainment. Her hair washed and hanging still damp down her back, she studied her face, looking for spots. There were none, she had a lovely skin which needed little make-up which was a good thing for she couldn't have afforded it anyway. Her hands needed attention, too...

She was ready long before she needed to be, her hair shining, her small nose powdered, sitting by the little fire with her skirts carefully spread out and Brimble perched carefully on her silken knee. A cheerful tattoo on the door sent her downstairs to open the door to discover that the same family who had taken her to the dance were calling for her. They greeted her with a good deal of friendly noise, waited while she fetched her coat and bade Brimble goodbye and wedged her on to the back seat between the two girls and drove off all talking at once. Such fun, she was told, just a few of us, nothing like the Christmas party but Mrs Bennett always has a splendid meal and lashings of drinks.

They sat down sixteen to dinner and Mary Jane found herself between two faces she recognised, the horsey Matt who it seemed was a nephew of Mrs Bennett's and the medical student, both of whom were in a festive mood and didn't lack for conversation. Dinner lasted a very long time and by the time they had had coffee it was getting on for eleven o'clock and more people were arriving. Mary Jane, listening to an elderly man with a very red face explaining the benefits of exactly the right mulch for roses, allowed her eyes to rove discreetly. It was silly, but she had hoped that perhaps Sir Thomas would be there…but he wasn't.

She was wrong. Calm and immaculate in his dinner-jacket, he arrived with five minutes to spare, just in nice time to take the glass of champagne he was offered and thread his way through the other guests to stand beside her.

CHAPTER SEVEN

MARY JANE saw him coming, and delight at seeing him again swamped every other feeling. She could feel herself going pale, as indeed she was, and her heart thumped so strongly that she trembled so that the glass she was holding wobbled alarmingly. He reached her side, took the glass from her and wished her good evening, adding, 'Did you think that I would not be here?'

He was smiling down at her and she only stopped herself just in time from telling him how wonderful it was to see him. She said instead, 'Well, it's a long way from London and I dare say you've been busy with your patients and—and had lots of invitations to spend the evening there.'

'Oh, yes, indeed, but I wished to spend the evening with my mother—she came over with me.'

She followed her train of thought. 'Isn't Felicity in London?'

He was still smiling but his eyes were cold. 'Yes, she sent you her love.' He might have added that she had wanted him to take her to a party at one of the big hotels and he had made the excuse that he was going to his mother's home. She had said sharply, 'How dull for you, Thomas. I don't suppose you'll see Mary Jane, but if you do or if you meet anyone who knows her send my love, will you?'

Mary Jane said in a wooden voice, 'It's a pity she isn't here...' She was unable to finish for there was

129

a sudden hush as Big Ben began to strike the hour. At its last stroke there were cries of 'Happy New Year!' as the champagne corks were popped and everyone started kissing everyone else. Mary Jane looked at the bland face beside her and said, meaning every word, 'I hope you have a very happy New Year, Sir Thomas.'

He smiled suddenly. 'I hope that we both shall, Mary Jane.' He bent and kissed her, a swift, hard kiss as unlike a conventional social peck as chalk from cheese. It took her breath but before she could get it back Matt had caught her by the hand and whirled her away to be kissed breathless by all the men there. She disentangled herself, laughing, and found Mrs Latimer standing close by.

'My dear, a happy New Year,' said Sir Thomas's mother, 'and how nice to see you enjoying yourself. You lead far too quiet a life.'

Mary Jane wished her a happy New Year in her turn. 'I've just been talking to Sir Thomas.' She blushed brightly, remembering his kiss, and Mrs Latimer just hid a smile.

'He drove down earlier this evening, and he will go back early tomorrow morning—he had made up his mind to be here.'

'He shouldn't work so hard,' said Mary Jane, and blushed again, much to her annoyance. 'What I mean is, he must get so tired.' She added, 'It's none of my business, please forgive me.'

'You're quite right,' observed Mrs Latimer. 'His work is his whole life although I think, when he marries, his wife and children will always come first.'

The very thought hurt; Mary Jane murmured suitably and said that she would have to find her hostess. 'Mrs Bennett kindly said that someone would drive me back as soon after midnight as possible.' She wished her companion goodbye and found Mrs Bennett at the far end of the room talking to Sir Thomas. As Mary Jane got within hearing, she said, 'There you are, my dear. What a pity that you must go but I quite understand...was it fun?'

'I've had a marvellous evening, Mrs Bennett, and thank you very much. I'll get my coat. Shall I wait in the hall and would it be all right if you said goodbye to everyone for me?'

'Of course, child. Sir Thomas is taking you home.'

'Oh, but Mrs Latimer is here, he'll—that is, you will have to come back for her.' She looked at him and found him smiling.

'The Elliots are driving her back presently.' He spoke placidly but she couldn't very well argue with him. She fetched her coat and got into the Rolls without speaking, only when they were away from the house and out of the village she said,

'I'm sorry to break up your evening.'

He said coolly, 'Not at all, Mary Jane, I had no intention of staying and it is only a slight detour to drop you off before I go back.'

A damping remark which she found difficult to answer but when the silence got too long she tried again. 'Did you bring Watson with you?'

'No—I'm only away for the night and I'll be back to take him for his run tomorrow before I go to my rooms. Tremble will look after him.'

'Won't you be tired?' She added hastily, 'I don't mean to be nosy.'

'I appreciate your concern. I'm not operating tomorrow and I have only a handful of private patients to see later in the day.'

The conversation, she felt, was hardly scintillating. The silence lasted rather longer this time. Presently she ventured, 'It was a very nice party, wasn't it?'

He said mildly, 'Do stop making light conversation, Mary Jane...'

'With pleasure,' she snapped. 'There is nothing more—more boring than trying to be polite to someone who has no idea of the social niceties.' She paused to draw an indignant breath, rather pleased with the remark, and then doubtful as to whether she had been rather too outspoken. His low laugh gave her no clue. She turned her head away to look out at the dark nothingness outside. Where was her good sense, she thought wildly; how could she have fallen in love with this taciturn man who had no more interest in her than he might have in a row of pins? She would forget him the moment she could get into her cottage and shut the door on him.

He drew up gently before her small front door, took the key from her hand and got out and opened it before coming back to open the door of the car for her.

Switching on the tea-room lights, he remarked, 'A cup of tea would be nice.'

'No, it wouldn't,' said Mary Jane flatly. 'Thank you for bringing me home, although I wish you hadn't.' She put a hand on the door, encouraging him to leave, a useless gesture since the door wasn't over-sturdy and his vast person was as unyielding as a tree trunk.

He laughed suddenly. 'Why do you laugh?' she asked sharply.

'If I told you you wouldn't believe me. Tell me, Mary Jane, why did you wish that I hadn't brought you home?'

She said soberly, 'I can't tell you that.' She held out a hand. 'I'm sorry if I've been rude.'

He took her hand between his. 'Goodnight, Mary Jane.' His smile was so kind that she could have wept.

He went out to his car and got in and drove away and she locked up and turned off the lights, gave Brimble an extra supper and took herself off to bed. It was another year, she thought, lying in bed, warmed by the hot water bottle and Brimble's small body. She wondered what it might bring.

It brought, surprisingly, Felicity, sitting beside a rather plump young man with bags under his eyes in a Mercedes. Felicity flung open the tea-shop door with a flourish. 'I just had to wish you a happy New Year,' she cried, and then paused to look around her. The little place was empty except for Mary Jane, who was on her knees hammering down a strip of torn lino by the counter. She got to her feet and turned round and the young man who had followed Felicity said, 'Good lord, is this your sister, darling?'

Mary Jane eyed him; this was not the beginning of a beautiful friendship, she reflected, but all the same she wished him good morning politely and kissed her sister's cheek. 'I'm spring cleaning,' she explained.

Felicity tossed off the cashmere wrap she had flung over her *haute couture* suit. 'Darling, how awful for you, isn't there a char or someone in this dump to do it for you?'

There didn't seem much point in answering that. 'Would you like a cup of coffee?' She waved at two chairs upended on to one of the tables. 'If you'd like to sit down it won't take long.'

Felicity said carelessly, 'This is Monty.' She went over to the table. 'Well, darling, give me a chair to sit on...'

Mary Jane thought that he didn't look capable of lifting a cup of tea let alone a chair and certainly he did it unwillingly. She went into the kitchen and collected cups and saucers while the coffee brewed and presently she went back to ask. 'Are you going somewhere or just driving round?'

'Riding round. It's very flat in town after New Year and I've no bookings until next week. Then it will be Spain, thank heaven. I need the sun and the warmth.'

Mary Jane let that pass, poured the coffee and took the tray across to the table and poured it for the three of them, rather puzzled as to why Felicity had come. She didn't have to wonder for long. 'Have you seen anything of Thomas?' asked Felicity. 'Well, I don't suppose you have but you may have heard something of him—after all, his mother doesn't live so far away, does she? She made a great fuss of you when you had the flu.'

She didn't wait for an answer, which was a good thing. 'I see quite a lot of him in town; I must say he's marvellous to go around with...'

'I say, steady on,' said Monty. 'I'm here, you know.'

Felicity gurgled with laughter. 'Of course you are, darling, and you're such fun.' She leaned across the table and patted his arm. 'But I do have my future to think of—a nice steady husband who adores me and can keep me in the style I've set my heart on...'

'You said you loved me,' complained Monty, and Mary Jane wondered if they had forgotten that she was there, sitting between them.

'Of course I do, Monty—marrying some well-heeled eminent surgeon won't make any difference to that.'

Mary Jane went into the kitchen. Felicity must be talking about Sir Thomas. If Felicity had been alone she might have talked to her about him and discovered if she were joking; her sister was selfish and uncaring of anyone but herself but there was affection between them; she could at least have discovered if she loved Sir Thomas. But the presence of Monty precluded that. She went back into the tea-room and found Felicity arranging the cashmere stole. 'Well, we're off, darling—lunch at that nice restaurant in Oxford, and then home to the bright lights.' She kissed Mary Jane. 'I'll send you a card from sunny Spain. I must try to see Thomas, I'm sure he could do with a day or two in the sun.'

Monty shook Mary Jane's hand. 'I would never have guessed that you two were sisters.' He shook his head, 'I mean to say...' He had a limp handshake.

Mary Jane put the 'Closed' sign on the door and went back to knocking in nails. Thoughts, most of them unhappy as well as angry, raced round her head. Surely, she told herself, Sir Thomas wasn't foolish enough to fall in love with Felicity, but of course if he really loved her—hadn't he said that loving and being in love were two different things? She forced herself to stop thinking about him.

After a few days customers began to trickle in; the Misses Potter came as usual for their tea and several ladies from the village popped in on their way to or from the January sales; life returned to its normal routine. Mary Jane sternly suppressed the thought of Sir Thomas, not altogether successfully, when a card from Felicity came. She had written on the back, 'Gorgeous weather, here for another week. Pity he has to return on Saturday. Be good. Felicity'.

Mary Jane ignored the last few words, she had no other choice but to be good, but, reading the rest of the scrawled words, she frowned. Felicity had hinted that she would see Sir Thomas and persuade him to go to Spain with her. It looked as though she had succeeded.

'I suppose the cleverer you are the sillier you get,' said Mary Jane in such a venomous tone that Brimble laid back his ears.

She was setting out the coffee-cups on Saturday morning when the first of the motorcyclists stopped before her door. He was joined by two others and the three of them came into the tea-room. Young men, encased in black leather and talking noisily. They took off their helmets and flung them down on one of the tables, pulled out chairs and sat down. They weren't local men and they stared at her until she felt uneasy.

'Coffee?' she asked. 'And anything to eat?'

'Coffee'll do, darlin', and a plate of whatever there is.' He laughed. 'And not much of that in this hole.' The other two laughed with him and she went into the kitchen to pour the coffee. Before doing so she picked up Brimble and popped him on the stairs and shut the door on him. She wasn't sure why she had done it; she wasn't a timid girl and the men would drink the coffee and go. She put the coffee on the table, then fetched a plate of scones and went back to the kitchen where she had been making pastry for the sausage rolls. She could see them from where she stood at the kitchen table and they seemed quiet enough, their heads close together, talking softly and sniggering. Presently they called for more coffee and ten minutes later they scraped back their chairs and put on their helmets. She took the bill over with an inward sigh of relief, but instead of taking it, the man she offered it to caught her hand and held it fast. 'Expect us to pay for that slop?' he wanted to know.

'Yes,' said Mary Jane calmly. 'I do, and please leave go of my hand.'

'Got a tongue in 'er 'ead, too. An' what'll you do if we don't pay up, Miss High and Mighty?'

'You will pay up. You asked for coffee and scones and I gave you them, so now you'll pay for what you've had.'

'Cor—got a sharp tongue, too, 'asn't she?' He tightened his grip. ''Ave ter teach 'er a lesson, won't we, boys?'

They swept the cups and saucers, the coffee-pot and the empty plates on to the floor and one of them went around treading on the bits of china, crushing them to fragments. The chairs went next, hurled across the room and then the tables. The little vases of dried flowers they threw at walls and all this was done without a word.

She was frightened but she was furiously angry too, she lifted a foot, laced into a sensible shoe, and kicked the man holding her hand. It couldn't have hurt much through all that leather, but it took him by surprise. He wrenched her round with a bellow of rage.

'Why, you little...'

Sir Thomas, on his way to spend a weekend with his mother and at the same time call upon Mary Jane, slowed the car as the tea-room came into view and then stopped at the sight of the motorbikes. He got out, saw the anxious elderly faces peering from the cottages on either side of Mary Jane's home, crossed the narrow pavement in one stride and threw open her door. A man who kept his feelings well under control, he allowed them free rein at the sight of her white face...

Mary Jane wished very much to faint on to a comfortable sofa, but she sidled to the remains of the counter and hung on to it. This was no time to faint; Sir Thomas had his hands full and apparently he was enjoying it, too. The little room seemed full of waving arms and legs. The man who had been holding her was tripped up neatly by one of Sir Thomas's elegantly shod feet and landed with a crash into the debris of tables and chairs which left Sir Thomas free to deal with the two other men. Subdued and scared by this large, silent man who knocked them around like ninepins, they huddled in a corner by their fallen comrade, only anxious to be left alone.

'Any one of you move and I'll break every bone in his body,' observed Sir Thomas in the mildest of voices, and turned his attention to Mary Jane.

His arm was large and comforting and as steady as a rock. 'Don't, whatever you do, faint,' he begged her, 'for there's nowhere for you to lie down.' Nothing in his kind, impersonal voice and his equally impersonal arm hinted at his great wish to pick her up and drive off with her and never let her go again. 'The police will be along presently; someone must have seen that something was wrong and warned them.' He looked down at the top of her head. 'I'll get a chair from the kitchen...'

She was dimly aware of someone coming to the door then, old Rob from his cottage by the church where he lived with his two sons. 'The Coats lad came running to tell something was amiss. The police is coming and my two boys'll be along in a couple of shakes.' He cast an eye over the three men huddled together. 'Varmints!' He turned a shrewd eye upon Sir Thomas. 'Knock 'em out, did yer? Nice bit of work, I'd say.'

The police, Rob's two sons and the rector arrived together. Not that Mary Jane cared. Let them all come, she reflected; a cup of tea and her bed was all she wanted. The bed was out of the question, but the rector, a meek and kindly man, made tea which she drank with chattering teeth, spilling a good deal of it, thankful that Sir Thomas was dealing with the police so that she needed to answer only essential questions before they marched the three men away to the waiting van. 'You'll need to come to the station on Tuesday morning, miss,' the senior office said. 'Nine o'clock suit you? Have you got a car?'

'I'll bring Miss Seymour, Officer,' said Sir Thomas and he nodded an affable goodbye and turned to old Rob. 'Will you wait while I see Mary Jane up to her bed?'

'I do not want...' began Mary Jane pettishly, not knowing what she was wanting.

'No, of course you don't.' Sir Thomas's voice was soothing. 'But in half an hour or so when you have got over the nasty shock you had, you will think clearly again. Besides, I want to have a look at that wrist.'

She went upstairs, urged on by a firm hand on her back, and found Brimble waiting anxiously on the tiny landing. The sight of his small furry face was too much; she burst into tears, sobbing and sniffing and grizzling into Sir Thomas's shoulder. He waited patiently until the sobs petered out, offered a handkerchief, observing that there was nothing like a good cry and at the same time tossing back the quilt on her bed.

'Half an hour,' he told her, tucking it around her and lifting Brimble on to the bed. 'I'll be back.'

Downstairs, he found old Rob and his sons waiting. 'Ah, yes, I wonder if I might have your help . . . ?' He talked for a few minutes and when old Rob nodded, money changed hands and they bade him goodbye and went off down the village street. Sir Thomas watched them go and then went to let the patient Watson out of the car and get his bag, let himself into the tea-room again and go soft-footed upstairs with Watson hard on his heels.

Mary Jane had fallen asleep, her hair all over the place, her mouth slightly open. She had a little colour now and her nose was pink from crying. Sir Thomas studied her lovingly and then turned his attention to her hand lying outside the quilt. The wrist was discoloured and a little swollen. The man's grasp must have been brutal. He suppressed the wave of rage which shook him and sat down to wait for her to wake up.

Which she did presently, the long lashes sweeping up to reveal the glorious eyes. Sir Thomas spent a few seconds admiring them. 'Better now? I'd like to take a look at that wrist. Does it hurt?'

'Yes.' she sat up in bed and dragged the quilt away. 'But I'm perfectly all right now. Thank you very much for helping me. I mustn't keep you . . .'

He was holding her hand, examining her wrist. 'This is quite nasty. I'll put a crêpe bandage on for the time being and we'll see about it later. Can you manage to pack a bag with a few things? I'm taking you to stay with my mother for a few days.'

She sat up very straight. 'I can't possibly, there's such a lot to do here, I must get someone to help me clear up and I must see about tables and chairs and cups and saucers and...' She paused, struck by the thought that she had no money to buy these essentials and yet she would have to have them, they were her very livelihood. She would have to borrow, but from whom? Oliver? Certainly not Oliver. Felicity? She might offer to help if she knew about it.

Sir Thomas, watching her, guessed her thoughts and said bracingly, 'There is really nothing you can do for a day or two.' He added vaguely, 'The police, you know. Far better to spend a little time making up your mind what is to be done first.'

'But your mother...'

'She will be delighted to see you again.' He got up and reached down the case on the top of the wardrobe. 'Is Brimble's basket downstairs? I'll get it while you pack—just enough for a week will do. Do you want to leave any messages with anyone? What about the milk and so on?'

'Mrs Adams next door will tell him not to call, and there's food in the fridge...'

'Leave it to me.'

She changed into her suit, packed the jersey dress, undies and a dressing-gown, her few cosmetics, then she did her hair in a perfunctory fashion and found scarf and gloves, out-of-date black court shoes, well-polished, and she burrowed in the back of a drawer and got the few pounds she kept for an emergency. By then, Sir Thomas was calling up the stairs to see if she was ready. He came to fetch her case while she picked up Brimble, carried him down to his basket and fastened him in. She was swept through the ruins of the tea-room before she had time to look round her, popped into the car with the animals on the back seat while he went back to lock the door. He came over to the car then. 'I think it might be a good idea to leave the key with Mrs Adams,' he suggested and she agreed readily, her thoughts busy with ways and means.

A tap on the window made her turn her head. The rector was there, so was his sister, Miss Kemble and Mrs Stokes and hurrying up the street was the shop-keeper. Mary Jane opened the window and a stream of sympathy poured in. 'If only we had known,' declared Miss Kemble, 'we could have come to your assistance.'

'But you did, at least the rector did. A cup of tea was exactly what I needed most! It was all a bit of a shock.'

The shopkeeper poked her head round Mrs Stokes' shoulder. 'A proper shame it is,' she declared. 'No one is safe these days. A good thing you've got the doctor here to take you to his mum. You 'ave a good rest, love—the place'll be as good as new again, don't you worry.'

They clustered round Sir Thomas as he came back to the car and after a few minutes' talk he got into his seat, lifted a hand in farewell and drove away. 'I like your rector,' he observed, 'but his sister terrifies me.'

Which struck her as so absurd that she laughed, which was what he had meant her to do.

He didn't allow her to talk about the disastrous morning either but carried on a steady flow of remarks to which, out of politeness, she was obliged to reply. When they arrived at his mother's house, she was met by that lady with sincere pleasure and no mention as to why she had come. 'We've put you in the room you had when you were here,' she was told. 'And have you brought your nice cat with you?'

Mrs Latimer broke off to offer a cheek to her son and receive Watson's pleased greeting. 'Would you like to go up to your room straight away? Lunch will be in ten minutes or so. Come down and have a drink first.'

The house was warm and welcoming and Mrs Beaver, coming into the hall, beamed at her with heart-warming pleasure. It was like coming home, thought Mary Jane, skipping upstairs behind that lady, only of course it wasn't, but it was nice to pretend...

No one mentioned the morning's events at lunch. The talk was of the village, a forthcoming trip Sir Thomas was to make to the Middle East and whether Mrs Latimer should go to London to do some shopping. Somehow they contrived to include Mary Jane in their conversation so that presently she was emboldened to ask, 'Are you going away for a long time?'

'If all goes well, I should be away for a week, perhaps less. I've several good reasons for wanting to get back as soon as possible.'

Was one of them Felicity? wondered Mary Jane, and Mrs Latimer put the thought into words by

asking, 'Have you seen anything of that glamorous sister of yours lately, Mary Jane?'

'No. I'm not sure where she is—she was in Spain but I don't know how long she will be there.'

Sir Thomas leaned back in his chair, his eyes on her face. 'Felicity is in London,' he observed casually.

It was quite true, thought Mary Jane, love did hurt, a physical pain which cut her like a knife. Somehow she was going to have to live with it. 'Perhaps you would like to go and see her?' Sir Thomas went on.

She spoke too quickly. 'No, no, there's no need, I mean, she's always so—that is, she works so hard she wouldn't be able to spare the time.'

She had gone rather red in the face and he said blandly, 'I don't suppose she could do much to help you,' and when his mother suggested that they have their coffee in the drawing-room she got up thankfully.

They had had their coffee and were sitting comfortably before the fire when Sir Thomas asked abruptly, 'Have you any money, Mary Jane?'

She was taken by surprise; there was no time to think up a fib and anyway, what would be the point of that? 'Well, no, I mean I have a few pounds—I keep them hidden at the cottage but I've brought them with me and there's about forty pounds in the post office.' She achieved a smile. 'I shall be able to borrow for the tea-room.' She added hastily, 'I'm not sure who yet, but I've friends in the village.'

'Good. As I said, there's nothing to be done for a day or two; besides, I think that wrist should be X-rayed. I'll take you up to town when I go on Monday morning—I'm operating all day but I'll bring you back in the evening. Someone can take you to

my house and Mrs Tremble will look after you until I'm ready.'

He smiled at her. 'You are about to argue but I beg you not to; I'm not putting myself out in the least.'

'It only aches a little.'

'You may have got a cracked bone.' He glanced at her bandaged wrist. He asked mildly, 'What had you done to annoy the man?'

'I kicked him.'

'Quite right too,' said Mrs Latimer. 'What a sensible girl you are. I would have done the same. Do you suppose it hurt?'

He went away presently to make some phone calls and Mrs Latimer said cosily, 'Now my dear, do tell me exactly what happened if you can bear to talk about it. What a brave girl you are. I should never have dared to ask for my money.'

So Mary Jane told her and discovered that talking about it made it seem less awful than she supposed. True, the problem of borrowing money and starting up again was at the moment impossible to solve but as her companion so bracingly remarked, things had a way of turning out better than one might expect. On this optimistic note she bore Mary Jane away to the conservatory at the back of the house to admire two camellias in full bloom.

The three of them had tea round the fire presently and sat talking until Sir Thomas was called to the phone and Mrs Latimer suggested that Mary Jane might like to unpack and then make sure that Mrs Beaver had prepared the right supper for Brimble, who had spent a day after his heart, curled up before the fire. Mary Jane went to her room, bearing him with her; there was some time before dinner and perhaps mother and son would like to be alone. So she stayed there, spending a lot of time before the looking-glass, trying out various hair-styles and then, disheartened by the fact that they didn't improve her looks in the slightest, pinning it in her usual fashion, applied lipstick and powder and, when the gong sounded, went downstairs, leaving Brimble asleep on the bed.

Sir Thomas and his mother were in the drawing-room and he got up at once and invited her to sit down and offered her a drink.

'But the gong's gone...'

He smiled. 'I don't suppose anything will spoil if we dine five minutes later. Did you fall asleep?'

He was making it easy for her and Mrs Latimer said comfortably, 'All that excitement—you must have an early night, my dear.'

They dined presently and Mary Jane discovered that she was hungry. The mushrooms in garlic sauce, beef Wellington and *crème brulée* were delicious and just right—as was the conversation; about nothing much, touching lightly upon any number of subjects and never once on her trying morning. As they got up from the table, Sir Thomas said casually,

'Shall we go for a walk tomorrow, Mary Jane? I enjoy walking at this time of year but perhaps you don't care for it?'

'Oh, but I do.' The prospect of being with him had sent the colour into her cheeks. 'I'd like that very much.'

'Good—after lunch, then. We go to church in the morning—come with us if you would like to.'

'I'd like that, too.'

'Splendid, I've fixed up an appointment for you on Monday morning—half-past nine—we'll have to leave around seven o'clock. I'm operating at ten o'clock.'

'I get up early. Would someone mind feeding Brimble? He'll be quite good on the balcony.'

'Don't worry about him, my dear.' Mrs Latimer was bending her head over an embroidery frame. 'Mrs Beaver and I will keep an eye on him. Thomas, did you bring any work with you?'

'I'm afraid so—there's a paper I have to read at the next seminar.'

'Then go away and read it or write it, or whatever you need to do. Mary Jane and I are going to have a nice gossip—I want to tell her all about Mrs Bennett's daughter—she's just got engaged . . .'

The rest of the evening passed pleasantly. Sir Thomas reappeared after an hour or so and shortly afterwards, in the kindest possible manner, suggested that she might like to go to bed. 'Rather a dull evening for you,' he apologised.

'Dull? It was heavenly.' Had he any idea what it was like to spend almost every evening on one's own even if one were making pastry or polishing tables and chairs? Well, of course he hadn't, he would spend his evenings with friends, going to the theatre, dining out and probably seeing as much of Felicity as possible. The sadness of her face at the thought caused him to stare at her thoughtfully. He wanted to ask her why she was sad, but, not liking him enough to answer, she would give him a chilly look from those lovely eyes and murmur something. He still wasn't sure if she liked him, and even if she did, she had erected an invisible barrier between them. He was going to need a great deal of patience.

She hadn't been expected to sleep but she did, to be wakened in the morning by Mrs Beaver with a tray of tea and the news that it was a fine day but very cold. 'Breakfast in half an hour, miss, and take my advice and wear something warm; the church is like an ice-box.'

She had brought her winter coat with her but it wouldn't go over her suit. It would have to be the jersey dress. She dressed under Brimble's watchful eye and went down to breakfast.

That night, curled up in her comfortable bed, she reviewed her day. It had been even better that she had hoped for. The three of them had gone to church and, despite the chill from the ancient building, she had loved every minute of the service, standing between Sir Thomas and his mother, and after lunch she had put on her sensible shoes, tied a scarf over her head and gone with him on the promised walk. It was a pity, she reflected, that they had talked about rather dull matters: politics, the state of the turnip crop on a neighbouring farm, the weather, Watson. She had wanted to talk about Felicity but she hadn't dared and since he hadn't mentioned the tea-room she hadn't liked to say anything about it. After all, he had done a great deal to help her; she was a grown woman, used to being on her own, capable of dealing with things like loans and painting and papering. Women were supposed to be equal to men now, weren't they? She didn't feel equal to Sir Thomas, but she supposed that she would have to do her best. He had been kind and friendly in a detached way but she suspected that she wasn't the kind of girl he would choose for a companion. She would have to go to London with him in the morning to have her wrist X-rayed, although it didn't seem necessary to her, but once she was back here she would go back to her cottage and then she need never see him again. She went to sleep then, feeling sad, and woke in the small hours, suddenly afraid of the future. It would be hard to begin again and it would be even harder never to see Sir Thomas, or worse—if he married Felicity, she would have to see him from time to time. She wouldn't be able to bear that, but of course she would have to. She didn't go to sleep again but lay making plans as to how to open the tea-room as quickly as possible with the least possible expense. She would need a miracle.

CHAPTER EIGHT

IT WAS still dark when they left the next morning. They had breakfast together, wasting no time and, with Watson drowsing on the back seat, had driven away, with no one but Mrs Beaver to see them off. Until they reached the outskirts of the city there was little traffic and they sat in a companionable silence, making desultory conversation from time to time. Crawling through the London streets, Mary Jane thanked heaven that she lived in the country. How could Felicity bear to live in the midst of all the noise and bustle? She asked abruptly, 'Do you like living in London?'

'My work is here, at least for a good part of the time. I escape whenever I can.'

They were in the heart of the city now and the hospital loomed ahead of them. At its entrance he got out, led her across the entrance hall and down a long tiled passage to the X-ray department, where he handed her over to a nurse.

'I'll see you later at my house,' he told her as he prepared to leave.

'Oh, won't you be here?' She was suddenly uncertain.

'I am going home now, but I shall be back presently. By then you will be taken care of by someone. Then Mrs Tremble is expecting you.'

She wanted to ask more questions, but the nurse was watching them with interest and besides, she could see that he was concealing impatience. She said goodbye and went with the nurse to take off her coat and have the bandage taken off her wrist.

The radiographer was young and friendly and she was surprised to find that he knew how her wrist had been injured. 'Sir Thomas phoned,' he told her airily, 'and of course he had to give me a history of the injury. Said you were a brave young lady. Does it bother you at all?'

'It aches but it doesn't feel broken.'

'There may be a bone cracked, though. Let's get it X-rayed—I'll get the radiologist to take a look at it and let Sir Thomas know as soon as possible.'

That done, he bade her goodbye, handed her over to the nurse to have the bandage put on again and then be taken back to the entrance hall.

There was a short, stout man talking to the porter but as she hesitated he came towards her. 'Miss Seymour, Sir Thomas asked me to drive you to his house. I'm Tremble, his butler.'

She offered a hand. 'Thank you, I'm afraid I'm being a nuisance...'

'Not at all, miss. You just come with me. Mrs Tremble has coffee waiting for you. Sir Thomas asked me to tell you that he may be delayed this evening and he hopes that you will dine with him before he drives you back to Mrs Latimer.'

He had ushered her out to the forecourt and into a Jaguar motor car, and as they drove away she asked, 'Where are we going?'

'To Sir Thomas's home, miss.' He had a nice fatherly manner. 'Me and my wife look after him, as you might say. Little Venice, that's where he lives, nice and quiet and not too far from the hospital.'

It wasn't the country, she reflected, but it was certainly quiet and even on a winter's day it was pleasant, with the water close by and the well-cared-for houses. Tremble ushered her in, took her coat and opened a door. Watson came to greet her as she went into the room.

She had found Mrs Latimer's house charming but this drawing-room was even more so. There were easy-chairs drawn up to a blazing fire, a vast sofa between them, covered as they were in a tawny red velvet. A Pembroke table stood behind it and on either wall were mahogany bow-fronted cabinets, filled with porcelain and silverware. At the window facing the street there was a Georgian library table, flanked by two side-chairs of the same period, and here and there, just where they would be needed, were tripod tables, bearing low table-lamps.

'Just you sit down,' said Tremble, 'and I'll bring you your coffee, miss.'

He went away, leaving her to inspect the room at her leisure with Watson pressed close to her, until she sat down in one of the chairs as Tremble came back. 'Sir Thomas said for you to make yourself at home, miss. There's the library across the hall if you should like to go there presently. Mrs Tremble will be along in a few minutes to make sure that what she's cooking for lunch suits you.'

'Please don't let her bother—I'm sure whatever it is will be delicious. I'm putting you to a great deal of trouble.'

'Not at all, miss. It's a pleasure to have you here. If Watson gets tiresome just open the French window and let him into the garden.'

Left alone, she drank her coffee, shared the biscuits with Watson and presently went to the French window at the back of the room to look out into the garden beyond. It was quite a good-sized garden with a high brick wall and, even on a grey winter day, was a pleasant oasis in the centre of the city. She went and sat down again and presently Mrs Tremble came into the room.

She was a tall, very thin woman with a sharp nose and a severe hairstyle, but she had a friendly smile and shrewd brown eyes. 'You'll be wanting to know where the cloakroom is, miss; I'm sure Tremble forgot to tell you. Forget his own head one day, he will! Now, as to your lunch; I've a nice little Dover sole and one of my castle puddings if that'll suit? Tremble will bring you a sherry and suggest a wine.'

So, later, Mary Jane sat down to her lunch and afterwards went to the library to choose something to read. The shelves were well-filled, mostly by ponderous volumes pertaining to Sir Thomas's work but she found a local history of that part of London and took it back to read by the fire. Her knowledge of London was scanty and it would be nice to know more about Sir Thomas's private life, even if it was only through reading about his house in a book.

Tremble brought her tea as dusk fell, and drew the red velvet curtains across the windows. 'I'll give Watson his tea now, miss, and take him for a quick run. When Sir Thomas is late home I do that, then the pair of them go for a walk later in the evening.'

Mary Jane ate her tea and, lulled by the warmth of the fire and the gentle lamp-light, she closed her eyes and went to sleep. Voices and Watson's bark woke her and she sat up as the door opened and Sir Thomas came in.

The thought of him had been at the back of her mind all day, mixed in with worried plans for the future of the tea-room. Now the sight of him, calm and self-assured, sent a wave of happiness through her insides.

She remembered just in time about Felicity and greeted him in a sober manner quite at variance with her sparkling eyes.

He wished her good evening in a friendly voice, enquired after her day and voiced the hope that she hadn't found it too tiresome that he had been delayed in driving her back to his mother's house.

'Tiresome? Heavens, no. I've had a lovely day. You can have no idea how delightful it is to eat a meal you haven't cooked for yourself. Such delicious food too! How lucky you are to have Mrs Tremble to cook for you, Sir Thomas—and I've done nothing all day, just lounged around with Watson.' She beamed at him. 'I expect you've been busy?'

He agreed that he had, in a bland voice which didn't betray a long session in Theatre, a ward round, outpatients clinic and two private patients he had seen when he should have been having lunch.

He had sat down opposite her. He had poured her a drink and was sitting with a glass of whisky on the table beside him. She looked exactly right sitting there in her unfashionable clothes; she would be nice to come home to. He dismissed the thought with a sigh; he wanted her for his wife, but only if she loved him, and he wasn't even sure if she liked him! She was grateful for his help, but gratitude was something he chose to ignore.

It was a pity that Mary Jane couldn't read his thoughts. She sat there, making polite conversation until Tremble came to tell them that dinner was served and at the table, sitting opposite him, she continued to make small talk while she ate her salmon mousse, beef *en croûte* and Mrs Tremble's lavish version of Queen of Puddings.

The excellent claret had loosened her tongue so that by the end of their meal she felt emboldened to ask, 'Will you be seeing Felicity? I expect——'

He said silkily, 'I do not know what you expect, Mary Jane, but rid yourself of the idea that I have any interest in your sister. Any meetings we have had have not been of my seeking.'

'Oh, I thought—that is, Felicity said . . . that you—that you got on well together.'

'In plain terms, that I had fallen in love with her, is that what you are trying to say?' He was suddenly coldly angry. 'You may believe me, Mary Jane, when I tell you that I have no wish to dangle after your sister. I am no longer a callow youth to be taken in by a pretty face.'

She had gone rather red. 'I'm sorry if I've annoyed you. It's none of my business,' and, at his questioning raised eyebrows, she added, 'your private life.'

He debated whether to tell her how mistaken she was and decided not to, and the conversation lapsed while Tremble brought in the coffee tray. When he had gone again, Mary Jane, for some reason, probably the claret, allowed her tongue to run ahead of her good sense. 'Haven't you ever been in love?' she wanted to know.

'On innumerable occasions from the age of sixteen or so. It is a normal habit, you know.'

'Yes, I know. I fell in love with the gym instructor when I was at school and then with the man who came to tune the piano at home. I actually meant enough to want to marry someone . . . ?'

He said gently, 'Yes, Mary Jane. And you?'

'Well, yes.'

'Still the piano-tuner?' He was laughing at her.

She said quickly, 'No,' and managed to laugh too; of course he had found her silly and rather rude, 'I dare say you're wedded to your work.' She spoke lightly.

'Certainly it keeps me fully occupied.' He glanced at his watch. 'Perhaps we had better go . . .'

She got up at once. 'Of course, I'm sorry, keeping you talking and you've had a long day already.'

She made short work of bidding the Trembles goodbye, saying just the right things in her quiet voice, shaking their hands and smiling a little when Tremble voiced the hope that he would see her again. 'Most unlikely.'

With Watson, drowsy after a good supper and a quick run, on the back seat, Sir Thomas drove away.

Mary Jane, still chatty from the claret, asked, 'Do you like driving?'

'Yes. It is an opportunity to think, especially at this time of night when the roads are fairly clear.'

She kept quiet after that. If he wanted to think then she wouldn't disturb him and if it came to that she had plenty to think about herself. She tore her eyes away from his hands on the wheel and stared ahead of her into the road, lit by the car's headlights. That way she could pretend that he wasn't there sitting beside her and concentrate on her own problems. When eventually he broke the silence it was to remind her that she had an interview with the police in the morning, something she had quite forgotten. 'I've arranged for an officer to come to Mother's house and interview you there,' he added.

'Thank you—I'd forgotten about it. Perhaps he could drive me back to the cottage? I really must start clearing up and getting it ready to open again.' A fanciful remark if ever there was one; she hadn't any idea at the moment how to find the money to start up once more, but he wasn't to know that.

Sir Thomas, who did know, gave a comforting rumble which might have meant anything and said briskly, 'Mother will be disappointed if you don't stay for a few days, and besides, although your wrist has no broken bones, it would be foolish of you to use it for anything more strenuous than lifting a tea-cup. Please do as I ask, Mary Jane, and wait another few days. If it won't bore you too much, I'll take you back home on Saturday morning.'

'Bored?' She was horrified at the thought. 'How could I possibly be bored in that lovely house, and your mother is so kind—I'd almost forgotten how nice mothers are.' There was a wistful note in her voice, and Sir Thomas sternly suppressed his wish to stop the car and comfort her in a manner calculated to make her forget her lack of a parent. Instead, he said in his quiet way, 'Good, that's settled, then.'

It was after ten o'clock when they reached Mrs Latimer's house and found the welcoming lights streaming from the windows and her waiting for them. So was the faithful Mrs Beaver, bustling in with a tray of coffee and sandwiches. 'And there's your bed waiting for you, Mary Jane, and you'd best be into

it seeing that Constable Welch'll be here at nine
o'clock sharp.'

Mary Jane drank her coffee obediently, ate a
sandwich and, although she very much wanted to stay
with Sir Thomas, bade them both goodnight.

'I dare say you'll be gone in the morning,' she
observed as they walked together to the door.

'I'll be gone in ten minutes or so,' he told her.

She stopped short. 'You're never going back now?
You can't—you mustn't, you've been at the hospital
all day and driven here and now you want to drive
straight back?'

He said placidly, 'I like driving at night and I
promise you I'll go straight to bed when I get home.'

She put a hand on his coat sleeve. 'You'll take care,
Thomas, do be careful.'

His eyes glinted under their lids. 'I'll be very careful,
Mary Jane.' He bent and kissed her then. It was a
quick, hard kiss, not at all like the very occasional
peck she received from friends. She didn't know much
about kisses, but this was definitely no peck. The look
she gave him was amethyst fire.

'Oh, Thomas,' she muttered, and flew across the
hall and upstairs, happily unaware that she had called
him Thomas twice. She woke in the night, however,
and she remembered. 'I am a fool,' she told Brimble,
curled up on her feet. 'What a good thing he's not
here and I must, simply must go away from here
before he comes again.'

She had no chance against Mrs Latimer's gentle in-
sistence that she should stay, or Mrs Beaver's more
emphatic opinion that she needed more flesh on her
bones and, over and above that, Constable Welch,
when he came, assured her that there was no need for

her return. 'Those men are to stay in custody for a
few more days until we get things sorted out,' he told
her. 'And there's nothing you can do for a bit.'

So she stayed in the nice old house, keeping Mrs
Latimer company, eating the nourishing food Mrs
Beaver insisted upon and discovering something of
Sir Thomas. For his mother was quick to show her
the family photo albums: Thomas as a baby, Thomas
as a boy, Thomas as a student, Thomas receiving a
knighthood...

'Why?' asked Mary Jane.

'Well, dear, he has done a great deal of work—
around the world, I suppose I could say—teaching
and getting clinics opened and lecturing, and, of
course, operating. His father was a surgeon, too, you
know.'

During the next few days she learnt a good deal
about Sir Thomas, information freely given by his
mother. By the time Saturday came around, Mary
Jane felt that she knew quite a lot about him. At least,
she told herself, she would have a lot to think about...

Watson's cheerful bark woke her the next morning
and a few minutes later Mrs Beaver came in with her
morning tea. 'He doesn't get enough rest,' she said,
as she pulled back the curtains, revealing a grey
February morning. 'Got here in the early hours, and
he's up and outside before I could put the kettle on.'
She shook her head. 'There's no holding him.'

When she had gone, Mary Jane got out of bed and
went to look out of the window. Sir Thomas was at
the end of the garden, throwing a ball for Watson.
Whatever Mrs Beaver thought, he appeared to be well-
rested and full of energy.

He wished her good morning with detached friendliness when she went down to breakfast, and asked if she would be ready to leave after breakfast and applied himself to his bacon and eggs. They had reached the toast and marmalade when he asked, casually, 'Have you any plans, Mary Jane?'

'I'll get cleared up,' she told him, summoning a cheerful voice. 'I can distemper the walls if they're marked, then I'll go to Cheltenham and borrow some money.' She didn't enlarge upon this and he didn't ask her to, which was just as well, because she had no idea how to set about it. She had spent several anxious hours during the nights going over her problems without much success and had come to the conclusion that if the solicitor who had attended to her uncle's affairs was unable to advise her there was nothing for it but to ask Felicity for some money.

They had almost finished when Mrs Latimer joined them. 'I shall miss you, dear,' she told Mary Jane. 'You must come and stay again soon— with Brimble, of course. Do take care of yourself. I shall come and see you and I'll bring Mrs Bennett with me.'

They left shortly after with Watson and Brimble sharing the back seat and Mary Jane very quiet beside Sir Thomas. There seemed nothing to say and since it was still only half light there was no point in admiring the scenery. It wasn't an awkward silence, though, she had the feeling that speech wasn't necessary, that he was content to drive silently, that to make conversation for its own sake was unnecessary. They were almost there when he observed casually, 'I shall be away all next week—Austria. I'll see you when I get back.'

He looked at her and smiled. It was a tender smile
and a little amused and she looked away quickly.
Then, for something to say, she asked, 'Have you been
to Austria before?'

'Several times. Vienna this time—a seminar there.'

He had slowed the car down the village street and
he stopped before her cottage, got out and opened the
door and let Watson out as he reached in for Brimble's
basket. Mary Jane stared.

'Someone's painted the outside—look...'

'So they have,' observed Sir Thomas, showing only
a faint interest as he took the key from a pocket and
opened the door.

She went in quickly and then stood quite still.
'Inside too,' she said. 'Look at the walls, and there's
a new counter and tables and chairs.' She turned to
look at him. 'Did you know? But how could...there's
no money to pay for it.' She stared into his quiet face.
'It's you, isn't it? You arranged it all.'

'Mr Rob and his sons have done all the work, your
friends in the village collected tables and chairs and
I imagine that every house in the village contributed
the china.'

'You arranged it, though, and you paid for it, too,
didn't you?' She smiled widely at him. 'Oh, Sir
Thomas, how can I ever thank you? And everyone
else of course, and as soon as I've got started again
I'll pay you back, every penny.'

'You called me Thomas.' He had come to stand very
close to her.

'I expect I forgot,' she told him seriously. 'I hope
you didn't mind.'

'On the contrary, I took it as a sign that we were
becoming friends.'

She put a hand on his arm. 'How can I ever be anything else after all you've done for me?' She reached up and kissed his cheek. 'I'll never forget you.'

'I rather hope you won't!'

He stared down at her with such intensity that she said hurriedly, 'Will you have a cup of coffee? It won't take a minute.'

He went to fetch her case from the car and she let an impatient Brimble out of his basket and put on the kettle and saw that there were cups and saucers arranged on the kitchen table and an unopened tin of biscuits, sugar in a bowl and milk in the fridge. She knew the reason a moment later for when Sir Thomas came in he was followed by the rector, his sister, old Rob and his sons, the shopkeeper and the Misses Potter.

There was a chorus of, 'Welcome back, Mary Jane,' and a good deal of talk and laughter as she made the coffee and handed round the cups. No one intended to hurry away; they all sat around, admiring their efforts, telling Mary Jane that she had never looked so plump and well. 'And we would never have done any of this if it hadn't been for Sir Thomas,' declared Miss Emily in her penetrating voice. 'He had us all organised in no time.'

It was a pity that presently he declared that he had to go and in the general bustle of handshaking and goodbyes Mary Jane had no chance to speak to him. She did go out to the car with him and stood there on the pavement, impervious to the cold, her hands held in his.

'We can't talk now, Mary Jane, and perhaps it is just as well, but I'm coming to see you. You want to see me, too, don't you?'

'Yes, oh, yes, please, Thomas!'

His kiss was even better than the last one. She stood there watching the Rolls disappear out of sight and would have probably gone on standing, freezing slowly, if Miss Kemble hadn't opened the door and told her to come inside at once. Mary Jane, who never took any notice of Miss Kemble's bossy ways, meekly did as she was told.

She was borne away presently to eat her lunch at the rectory and to be given a great deal of unheeded advice by Miss Kemble. That lady said to her brother later in the day, 'I have never known Mary Jane to be so attentive and willing to take my advice.'

Mary Jane had heard perhaps one word in ten of Miss Kemble's lectures; her head was full of Sir Thomas, going over every word he had said, the way he had looked, his kiss.

Back in her cottage once more, she assured Brimble that she would be sensible, at least until she saw him again. He had said that he wanted to see her again... she forgot about being sensible and fell to daydreaming again.

She was up early the next morning, polishing and dusting, setting out cups and saucers and making a batch of scones. Sunday was a bad day usually, and she seldom opened, only in the height of the tourist season, but she had a feverish wish to get back to her old life as quickly as possible. Her efforts were rewarded, for several cars stopped and when she opened again after lunch there were more customers. It augured well for the future, she told herself, counting the takings at the end of the afternoon.

Her luck held for the first few days, and a steady trickle of customers came; if it continued so, she could make a start on paying back Sir Thomas. She had no idea how much it would be and probably she would be in his debt for years.

Thursday brought Oliver. He marched into the tea-room and stood looking around him. 'Who paid for all this?' he wanted to know.

Mary Jane, her hands floury from her pastry making, stood in the kitchen doorway, looking at him. 'So you did hear about the—incident? The rector told me that he had let you know...'

Oliver blew out his cheeks. 'Naturally, it was his duty to inform me.'

Mary Jane put her neat head on one side. 'And what did you do about it?'

'There was no necessity for me to do anything. The place was being put to rights.' He looked around him. 'It must have cost you a pretty penny. You borrowed, of course?'

'That's my business. Have you just come to see if I'm still here or do you want something?'

'Since your regrettable treatment of Margaret I would hesitate to ask any favours of you.'

'Quite right too, Oliver. So it's just curiosity.'

He said pompously, 'I felt it my duty to come and see how things were.'

'Oh, stuff,' said Mary Jane rudely. 'Do go away, Oliver, you're wasting my time.'

'You've wasted enough time with that surgeon,' he sneered. 'We hear the village gossip as well as everyone else. Hoping to catch him, are you? Well, I'll tell you something—even if you were pretty, and knew how to dress you wouldn't stand a chance. That sister of yours has him hooked. We've been to town and met her—just back from Vienna. She means to marry him, and I must say this for the girl, she always gets what she wants.'

She put her hands behind her back because they were shaking and, although she had gone pale, she said steadily enough, 'Felicity is beautiful and famous and she works hard at her job. She deserves to have whatever she wants.'

'Well, from all accounts he's a great catch— loaded, well-known and handsome. What more could a girl want?' He laughed nastily. 'So you can stop your silly dreaming and look around for someone who's not too fussy about looks.'

'Oh, do go. I'm busy.' She added, 'You're getting fat, Oliver—you ought to go on a diet.'

If he didn't go quickly, she reflected, she would scream the place down. He was sly and mean and she had no doubt at all that he had come intending to tell her about Felicity and Sir Thomas; he had obviously known all about the tea-room being vandalised and what Sir Thomas had done to help her. Thankfully, he went with a last, sniggering, 'I don't expect Felicity will ask you to be a bridesmaid, but you wouldn't like that, would you? Seeing the man of your dreams marrying your sister.'

It was too much; she had been cutting up lard to make the puff pastry for the sausage rolls, and she scooped up a handful and threw it at him as he opened the door. It caught him on the side of his head and slid down his cheek, oozed over his collar and down on to his overcoat.

Rage and surprise rendered him speechless. 'Bye bye, Oliver,' said Mary Jane cheerfully.

She locked the door when he had gone, turned the sign to 'Closed' and went upstairs where she sat down and had a good cry. It had been foolish of her, she told Brimble, to imagine, even for a moment, that Sir Thomas had any deeper feelings for her than those of friendliness and—regrettably—pity, but he could have told her ... and he was coming to see her; he wanted to talk. Well, of course he did, he wanted to tell her about Felicity and himself, didn't he? But why couldn't he have told her sooner and only kissed her in a casual manner, so that she couldn't get silly ideas into her head? She blew her red nose, bathed her eyes and went back to her pastry making. Perhaps Oliver had been lying; he was quite capable of that. The thought cheered her so that by the time she had taken the sausage rolls from the oven she felt quite cheerful again.

She had some more customers calling in for coffee and sausage rolls. Several of them remarked upon her heavy cold and she agreed quickly, conscious that her eyes were still puffy and her nose still pink.

Sir Thomas had thoughtfully caused a telephone to be installed when the tea-room had been done up, arguing that as she lived alone it was a sensible thing to have. She had thanked him nicely, wondering how she was going to pay for its rental, let alone any calls she might make.

When it rang just before closing time she lifted the receiver—only he and possibly Mrs Latimer would know the number and, even if her friends in the village knew it, too, they would hardly waste money ringing her up when they only needed to nip down the road. 'Thomas,' she said happily to Brimble, disturbed from a refreshing nap.

It was Felicity.

'Felicity,' said Mary Jane. 'How did you know I had a phone?'

'Thomas told me. Back with your nose to the pastry-board again? What a thrill for you, darling. I'm just back from Vienna and in an absolute daze of happiness, darling. I told you I'd marry when I found the right man—good looks, darling, lots of lovely money and dotes on me.'

Mary Jane found her voice. 'What wonderful news and how exciting. When will you get married?'

'I've one or two modelling dates I can't break but very soon—a few weeks. I wanted to move in with him, but he wouldn't hear of it.' She giggled. 'He's very old-fashioned.'

Mary Jane wasn't sure about Sir Thomas being old-fashioned but she was quite sure that allowing Felicity to move in with him would be something he would never agree to.

'Will you have a big wedding?'

'As big as I am able to arrange in a few weeks. There's a nice little church close by—we've dozens of friends between us and I shall wear white, of course. Bridesmaids, too. A pity you're so far away, darling.'

Which remark Mary Jane took, quite rightly, to be a kinder way of saying that she wasn't expected to be a bridesmaid or even a guest.

'What would you like for a wedding present?'

Felicity laughed. 'Oh, darling, don't bother, I'm sending a list to Harrods. Besides, you haven't any money.'

Mary Jane was pleased to hear how bright and cheerful her voice sounded. 'Let me know the date of the wedding, anyway,' she begged. 'And I'm so glad you're happy, dear.' She was going to burst into tears any minute now. 'I must go, I've scones in the oven.'

'You and your scones,' laughed Felicity, and rang off. Just in time. She locked the door and turned the notice round and switched off the lights, not forgetting to put the milk bottles outside the back door and check the fridge before polishing the tables ready for the morning. All the while she was weeping quietly. Oliver, with his nasty, snide remarks, had been bad enough and she had almost persuaded herself that he had just been malicious, but now Felicity had told her the same story.

Moping would do no good, she told herself presently, and started to clean the stove—a job she hated, but anything was better than having time to think.

She pushed her supper round and round her plate and went to bed. It was a well-known adage that things were always better in the morning.

They were exactly the same, except that now she never wanted to see Thomas again. He had been amusing himself while Felicity was away, playing at being the Good Samaritan. She ground her little white teeth at the thought. If it took her the rest of her life she would pay him back every penny. How dared he kiss her like that, as though he actually wanted to...?

He had said that he would be away for the whole of the week and it was still only Friday; she would have the weekend to decide how she would behave and even if he had to go to the hospital or see his patients he might not come for some days. He might not come at all.

'Which, of course, would be far the best thing,' she told Brimble.

He came the next day just as she was handing a bill to the last of the few people who had been in for tea. She stared at him across the room, her heart somersaulting against her ribs. He looked as he always did, calm and detached, but he was smiling a little. Well he might, reflected Mary Jane, ushering her customers out of the door which Sir Thomas promptly closed, turning the sign round.

'It is not yet five o'clock,' said Mary Jane frostily. Talking to him wasn't going to be difficult at all because she was so angry.

'I got back a day early,' said Sir Thomas, still standing by the door. 'It has been a long week simply because I want to talk to you.'

'Well, you need not have hurried. Felicity phoned me. She's—she's very happy, I hope you will be too.' Despite her efforts her voice began to spiral. 'You could have told me . . . You've been very kind, more than kind, but I can understand that you wanted to please her.'

'What exactly are you talking about?' he wanted to know, his voice very quiet.

'Oh, do stop pretending you don't know,' she snapped. 'I knew that you would fall in love with her but you didn't tell me, you let me think . . . did you have a nice time together in Vienna?'

His voice was still quiet but now it was cold as well. 'You believe that I went straight from you to be with Felicity? That I am going to marry her? That I was amusing myself with you?'

'Of course I do. Oliver told me and I didn't quite believe him and then she phoned.'

'Is that what you think of me, Mary Jane?' And when she nodded dumbly he gave her a look of such icy rage that she stepped back. If only he would go, she thought miserably, and had her wish.

CHAPTER NINE

MARY JANE stood in the middle of the sitting-room, listening to the faint whisper of the Rolls-Royce's departure, regretting every word she had uttered. She hadn't given Sir Thomas a chance to speak, and her ingratitude must have shocked him. She should have behaved like a future sister-in-law, congratulated him and expressed her delight. All she had done was to let him see that she had taken him seriously when all the time he was merely being kind. Well, it was too late now. She had cooked her goose, burnt her boats, made her bed and must lie on it. She uttered these wise sayings out loud, but they brought her no comfort.

She felt an icy despair too deep for tears. The thought of a lifetime of serving tea and coffee and baking cakes almost choked her. She could, of course, sell the cottage and go right away, but that would be running away, wouldn't it? Besides, she must owe him a great deal of money...

Leaving church the next morning, Miss Kemble took her aside. 'You must have your lunch with us,' she insisted, overriding Mary Jane's reasons for not doing so. 'Of course you must come, you are still too pale. Do you not sleep? Perhaps you are nervous of being alone?'

Mary Jane said very quickly that she wasn't in the least nervous—only at the thought of Miss Kemble moving in to keep her company. 'Besides,' she pointed out, 'I have a telephone now.'

'Ah, yes, that charming Sir Thomas Latimer, what a good friend he has been to you. I hear from all sides how thoughtful he is of others—always helping lame dogs over stiles.' An unfortunate remark unintentionally made.

They were kind at the rectory. She was given a glass of Miss Kemble's beetroot wine and the rector piled her plate with underdone roast beef which she swallowed down, wishing that Brimble were there to finish it for her. I don't mean to be ungrateful, she reflected, but why does Miss Kemble always make me feel as if I were an object for charity?

She left shortly after their meal with the excuse that she intended to go for a brisk walk. 'For I don't get out a great deal,' she explained, and then wished that she hadn't said that, for Miss Kemble might decide to go with her.

However, there was a visiting parson coming to tea and staying the night, so Miss Kemble was fully occupied. Mary Jane thanked the pair of them sincerely; they had been kind and going to the rectory had filled in some of the long day. Sunday was always a bad day with time lying heavy on her hands, and today was worse than usual. She tired herself out with a long walk; as the days went by it would get easier to forget Sir Thomas and the chances of seeing much of him were slight; Felicity didn't like a country life. She let herself into her cottage, shed her coat and scarf, fed Brimble and spent a long time cooking a supper she hardly touched.

There was a spate of customers on Monday morning to keep her busy and she had promised to make a cake for the Women's Institute meeting during the week, so the baking of it took most of the afternoon.

'Another day gone,' said Mary Jane to Brimble.

Mrs Latimer and Mrs Bennett came the next day. 'We thought we would have a little drive round, dear,' explained Mrs Latimer, 'and we'd love a cup of coffee.'

They sat down, her only customers—and begged her to join them.

'I must say I'm disappointed,' observed Mrs Latimer. 'You don't look at all well, dear. You were quite bonny when I last saw you. Are you working too hard? A few days' rest perhaps? Thomas is back from wherever it was he went to...'

'Vienna.'

'That's right. Has he been to see you?'

Mrs Latimer's blue eyes were guileless.

'Yes.'

For the life of her, Mary Jane couldn't think of anything to add to that. And if Mrs Latimer expected it she gave no sign but made some observation about the life her son led. 'It is really time he settled down,' she declared, which gave Mrs Bennett the chance to talk about her recently engaged daughter, so that any chance Mary Jane had of finding out more about Thomas and Felicity was squashed.

'You must come and see us,' said Mrs Bennett. 'On a Sunday, when you're free. How nice that you're on the telephone—very thoughtful of Thomas to have it put in. I must say it has all been beautifully redecorated.'

'He's been very kind,' said Mary Jane woodenly. 'And the village gave me the china and the tables and chairs. I don't think I could have managed to start again without help. I'm very grateful.'

'My dear child,' said Mrs Latimer, 'I don't know of many girls who would have carved themselves a living out of an old cottage and the pittance your uncle left you, and as for that wretched cousin of yours...'

'I don't see Oliver very often,' said Mary Jane, adding silently, Only when he wants something or has news which he knows might upset me.

The two ladies left presently and, save for a man on a scooter who had taken a wrong turning, she had no more customers that day.

Sir Thomas immersed himself in his work, as calm and courteous and unflappable as he always was, only Tremble was disturbed. 'There's something up,' he confided to Mrs Tremble. 'Don't ask me what, for I don't know, but there's something wrong somewhere.'

'That nice young lady...' began his wife.

'Now don't go getting sentimental ideas in your head,' begged Tremble.

'Mark my words,' said Mrs Tremble, who always managed to have the last word.

That same evening Felicity arrived on Thomas's doorstep. Tremble, opening the door to her, tried not to look disapproving; he didn't like flighty young ladies with forward manners but he begged her to go into the small sitting-room behind the little dining-room while he enquired if Sir Thomas was free.

Thomas was at his desk writing, with Watson at his feet. He looked up with a frown as Tremble went in. 'Something important, Tremble?'

'A young lady to see you, sir, a Miss Seymour.'

The look on his master's face forced him to remember his wife's words. If this was the young lady who was giving all the trouble then he for one was disappointed. There was no accounting for taste, of course, but somehow she didn't seem right for Sir Thomas.

He followed his master into the hall and opened the sitting-room door and let out a sigh of relief when Sir Thomas exclaimed, 'Felicity—I thought it was Mary Jane.'

'Mary Jane? Whatever would she be doing in London? You might at least look pleased to see me, Thomas. I've news for you—it will be in the papers tomorrow but I thought you might like to know before then. I'm engaged, isn't it fun? A marvellous man— a film director, no less. I've had him dangling for weeks—a girl has to think very carefully about her future, after all. He went to Vienna with me and I decided he'd do. He is in the States now, coming back tomorrow. You'll come to the wedding, of course. I phoned Mary Jane—she won't be coming, she'd be like a fish out of water and she hasn't the right clothes.'

Sir Thomas was still standing, looking down at her, sitting gracefully in a high-backed chair. He said evenly, 'I think it is unlikely that I shall be free to come to your wedding, Felicity. I hope that you will both be very happy. I expect Mary Jane was surprised.'

Felicity shrugged. 'Probably. You were in Vienna, too, were you not? We might have met but I suppose you were lecturing or something dull.'

'Yes. May I offer you a drink?'

'No, thanks, I'm on my way to dine with friends.' She smiled charmingly. 'Do you know, Thomas, I considered you for a husband for a while but it would never have done; all you ever think of is your work.'

He smiled. He didn't choose to tell her how mistaken she was.

On Thursday afternoon the Misses Potter came for tea, as usual. There had been a handful of customers but now the tea-room was empty and Miss Emily said in a satisfied voice, 'I am glad to find that you have no one else here, Mary Jane, for we have brought the newspaper for you to read. There is something of great interest in it. Of course, the *Telegraph* only mentions it, but I persuaded Mrs Stokes to let me have her *Daily Mirror* which has more details.'

The ladies sat themselves down at their usual table and Mary Jane fetched tea and scones and waited patiently while the ladies poured their tea and buttered their scones. This done, Miss Emily took the newspapers from her shopping basket and handed them to her. The *Telegraph* first, the page folded back on 'Forthcoming Marriages'.

Mary Jane's eyes lighted on the announcement at once. 'Mr Theobald Coryman, of New York, to Miss Felicity Seymour of London.' She read it twice just to make sure, and then said, 'I don't understand—is it a mistake?'

'In the *Telegraph*?' Miss Emily was shocked. 'A most reputable newspaper.' She handed over the *Daily Mirror*, which confirmed the *Telegraph*'s genteel announcement in a more flamboyant manner. 'Famous Model to Wed Film Director' said the front-page and under that a large photo of Felicity and a man in horn-rimmed glasses and a wide-brimmed hat. They were arm in arm and Felicity was displaying the ring on her finger.

'It must be a mistake,' said Mary Jane. 'Felicity said...!'

She remembered with clarity what her sister had said—word for word, and Thomas's name had not been mentioned. It was she herself who had made the mistake, jumped to the wrong conclusion and accused Sir Thomas of behaviour in a manner which had been nothing short of that of a virago. She had indeed cooked her goose; worse, she had wronged him in a manner he wasn't likely to forgive or forget. She hadn't given him a chance to say anything, either.

The Misses Potter were looking at her in some astonishment. 'You are pleased? Felicity seems to have done very well for herself.'

'Yes, I'm delighted,' said Mary Jane wildly. 'It's marvellous news. I'm sure she'll—they—will be very happy. He looks...!' She paused, at a loss to describe her sister's future husband; there wasn't much of him to see other than the hat and the glasses. 'Very nice,' she finished lamely.

'They seem very suitable,' remarked Miss Emily drily. 'He is, so they say, extremely rich.'

'Yes, well, Felicity likes nice things.'

The elderly sisters gave her a thoughtful glance. 'I think we all do, dear,' said Miss Mabel. 'You look a bit peaked—have a cup of tea with us.'

Which Mary Jane did; a cup of tea was the panacea for all ills, at least in the United Kingdom, and it gave her time to pull herself together.

The Misses Potter went presently, and she was left with her unhappy thoughts. Would it be a good idea, she wondered, to write to Sir Thomas and apologise; on the other hand, would it be better to do nothing about it? Had she the courage, she wondered, to write and tell him that she loved him and would he forgive her? She went upstairs and found paper and pen and sat down to compose a letter. An hour later, with the wastepaper basket overflowing, she gave up the attempt. Somehow her feelings couldn't be expressed with pen and ink. 'In any case,' she told Brimble, 'I don't suppose he has given me a thought.'

In this she was mistaken; Sir Thomas had thought about her a great deal. Although he shut her away to the back of his mind while he went about his work, sitting in Sister's office after a ward round, apparently giving all his attention to her tart remarks about lack of staff, the modern nurse, the difficulties she experienced in getting enough linen from the laundry—all of which he had heard a hundred times before, he was thinking that he would like to wring Mary Jane's small neck and then, illogically, toss her into his car and drive away to some quiet spot and marry her out of hand. How dared she imagine for one moment that he was amusing himself with her when he loved her to distraction? That he had never allowed his feelings to show was something he hadn't considered.

He promised Sister that he would speak to the hospital committee next time it met, and wandered off to be joined presently by his registrar wanting his opinion about a patient. Stanley Wetherspoon was a good surgeon and his right hand, but a bit prosy. Halfway through his carefully expressed opinion, Sir Thomas said suddenly, 'Why didn't I think of it before? Of course, we were in Vienna at the same time. Naturally...'

Stanley paused in mid-flow and Sir Thomas said hastily, 'So sorry, I've lost the thread—this prosthesis—what do you suggest that we do?'

Presently, Stanley went on his way, reassured, wondering all the same if his boss was overworking and needed a holiday.

Sir Thomas, outwardly his normal pleasantly assured self, went to his rooms, saw several patients and then requested Miss Pink to come into his consulting-room.

'How soon can I get away for a day?'

'Well, it's your weekend on call, Sir Thomas—I could ask your patients booked for Monday to come on Saturday morning—since you'll be here anyway—if you saw them then you could have Monday off.'

'And Tuesday? I know I've got a couple of cases in the afternoon, but is the morning free?'

'It will be if I get Mrs Collyer and Colonel Gregg to come in the afternoon—after three o'clock? That'll give you time to get back to your rooms from hospital and have a meal.'

'Miss Pink, you are a gem of real value to me. Do all that, will you? Then let me know when you've fixed things.'

At the door she asked, 'You'll leave an address, Sir Thomas?'

'Yes. I'll go very early in the morning; if you need anything, get hold of Tremble.'

'Well, well,' said Miss Pink, peering out of the window to watch him getting into his car, and she went in search of his nurse, tidying up in the examination-room. A lady of uncertain age, just as she was, and devoted, just as she was, to Sir Thomas's welfare.

'He looked so happy,' said Miss Pink, and, after a cosy chat of a romantic nature, she went away to re-organise his days for him. A task which necessitated a good deal of wheedling and coaxing, both of which she did most willingly; Sir Thomas had the gift of inspiring loyalty and, in Miss Pink's case, an abiding devotion.

Mary Jane spent the next three days composing letters in her head to Sir Thomas, but somehow when she wrote them down they didn't seem the same. By Sunday evening she had a headache, made worse by a visit from Oliver.

'Well, what do you think of Felicity?' he wanted to know when she opened the door to him.

'I'm very pleased for her, Oliver. You had it all wrong, didn't you?'

He gave her a nasty look. 'I may have been mistaken with the name of her future husband, but there's no denying that she has done very well for herself.'

'Why have you come?' asked Mary Jane, not beating about the bush and anxious for him to go again.

'Margaret and I have had a chat—now that this place is tarted up and equipped again, we think that it might be a good idea if we were to buy you out. You can stay here, of course—the cottage is yours anyway, more's the pity—you can run the place and we will pay you a salary. A little judicial advertising and it should make it worth our while.' He added smugly, 'We can use the connection with Felicity—marvellous publicity.'

'Over my dead body,' said Mary Jane fiercely. 'Whatever will you dream up next? And, if that is why you came, I'll not keep you.'

She opened the door and ushered him out while he was still arguing.

When he had gone, however, she wondered if that wouldn't have solved her problem. Not that she would have stayed in the cottage. There was no doubt that he would buy the place from her even if it meant getting someone in to run it. She would have money and be free to go where she wanted. She couldn't think of anywhere at the moment, but no doubt she would if she gave her mind to it. The trouble was, she thought only of Sir Thomas.

The sun was shining when she got up on Monday morning; February had allowed a spring day with its blue sky and feathery clouds to sneak in. Mary Jane turned the door sign to 'Open', arranged cups and saucers on the four tables and made a batch of scones. The fine weather might tempt some out-of-season tourist to explore and come her way. Her optimism was rewarded: first one table, then a second and finally a third were occupied. Eight persons drinking coffee at fifty-five pence a cup and eating their way through the scones. She did some mental arithmetic, not quite accurate, but heartening none the less, and made plans to bake another batch of scones during the lunch hour. It was still only mid-morning and there might be other customers.

The family of four at one of the tables called for more coffee and she was pouring it when the door opened and Sir Thomas came in, Watson at his heels. It was difficult not to spill the coffee, but she managed it somehow, put the percolator down on the table and, heedless of the customers' stares, stood gaping at him. He sat down at the remaining empty table, looking quite at his ease, and requested coffee. Watson, eager to greet Mary Jane, had, at a quiet word from his master, subsided under the table. Sir Thomas nodded vaguely at the other customers and looked at Mary Jane as though he had never seen her before, lifting his eyebrows a little because of her tardy response to his request.

The wave of delight and happiness at the sight of him which had engulfed her was swamped by sudden rage. How could he walk in as though he were a complete stranger and look through her in that casual manner? Coffee, indeed. She would like to throw the coffee-pot at him...

She poured his coffee with a shaky hand, not looking at him but stooping to pat the expectant Watson's head, and then, just to show him that he was only a customer like anyone else, she made out the bill, laid it on the table and held out her hand for the money.

He picked the hand up gently. It was a little red and rough from her chores, but it was a pretty shape and small. He kissed it on its palm and folded her fingers over it and gave the hand back to her.

What would have happened next was anybody's guess, but the two women who had arrived in a small car, having taken a wrong turning, asked loudly for their bill. When they had gone, Mary Jane made herself as small as possible behind the counter, taking care not to look at Sir Thomas, very aware that he was looking at her. The young couple on a walking holiday went next, looking at her curiously as they went out, frankly staring at Sir Thomas, and that left the family of four, a hearty, youngish man, his cheerful loud-voiced wife and two small children. They had watched Sir Thomas with avid interest, in no hurry to be gone, hoping perhaps for further developments. Sir Thomas sat, quite at his ease, silent, his face a blank mask, his eyes on Mary Jane. Unable to spin out their meal any longer, they paid their bill and prepared to go. His wife, looking up from fastening the children's coats, beamed at Mary Jane. 'You'll be glad to see the back of us, love—I dare say he's dying to pop the question—can't take his eyes off you, can he?'

They all went to the door and she turned round as they went out. 'Good luck to you both, bye bye.'

They got into their car and Sir Thomas got up, turned the sign to 'Closed', locked the door and stood leaning against it, his hands in his pockets.

Mary Jane, standing in the middle of the room, waited for him to speak; after a while, when the silence became unbearable, she said the first thing to come into her head.

'Shouldn't you be at the hospital?'

'Indeed I should, but, owing to Miss Pink's zealous juggling of my appointments book, I have given myself the day off.' He smiled suddenly and her heart turned over. 'To see you, my dearest Mary Jane.'

'Me?'

'You believed that I had gone to Vienna to be with Felicity?' He asked the question gravely.

'Well, you see, Oliver told me and then Felicity phoned and she didn't say who it was and I thought it would be you—she said you were famous and rich and good-looking and you are, aren't you? It sounded like you.'

'And then?' he prompted gently.

'Miss Emily showed me two newspapers and one of them had a photo of Felicity and—I've forgotten his name, but he wears a funny hat, and I tried to write you a letter but it was too difficult...'

'You supposed that I had helped you to set this place to rights because you are Felicity's sister?'

She nodded. 'I was a bit upset.'

'And why were you upset, Mary Jane?'

She met his eyes with an effort. 'I'd much rather not say, if you don't mind.'

'I mind very much. I mind about everything you say and do and think. I am deeply in love with you, my dearest girl, you have become part—no, my whole life. I want you with me, to come home to, to talk to, to love.'

Mary Jane was filled with a delicious excitement, and a thankful surprise that sometimes dreams really did come true. She said in a small voice, 'Are you quite sure, Thomas? I love you very much, but Oliver...'

Sir Thomas left the door and caught her close. 'Oliver can go to the devil. Say that again, my darling.'

She began obediently, 'Are you quite sure...?' She peeped at him and saw the look on his face. 'I love you very much.'

'That's what I thought you said, but I had to make sure.'

'But I must tell you...'

'Not another word,' said Sir Thomas, and kissed her. Presently, Mary Jane, a little out of breath, lifted her face to his. 'That was awfully nice,' she told him.

'In which case...'

'Thomas, there's a batch of scones in the oven.' She added hastily, 'It isn't that I don't want you to kiss me, I do, very much, but they'll burn.'

Sir Thomas, quite rightly, took no notice of this remark but presently he said, 'Pack a bag, my love, and urge Brimble into his basket. You may have ten minutes. I will see to things here. No, don't argue, there isn't time—you may argue as much as you wish once we're married.'

She reached up and kissed his chin. 'I'll remember that,' she said and slipped away up the stairs to do as she was told.

He watched her go before going into the kitchen and rescuing the scones, the faithful Watson beside him. Brimble was on the kitchen table, waiting.

'What must I take with me, Thomas?' Mary Jane's voice floated down the little stairs. 'You didn't say where we are going?'

He stood looking up at her anxious face. 'Why, home, of course, my love.' And saw her lovely smile.

INSTANT WIN 4229 SWEEPSTAKES
OFFICIAL RULES

1. NO PURCHASE NECESSARY. YOU ARE DEFINITELY A WINNER. For eligibility, play your instant win ticket and claim your prize as per instructions contained thereon. If your "Instant Win" ticket is missing or you wish another, send a self-addressed, stamped envelope (WA residents need not affix return postage) to: Instant Win 4229 Ticket, P.O. Box 9045, Buffalo, NY 14269-9045 in the U.S., and in Canada, P.O. Box 609, Fort Erie, Ontario, L2A 5X3. Only one (1) "Instant Win" ticket will be sent per outer mailing envelope. Requests received after 12/30/96 will not be honored.

2. Prize claims received after 1/15/97 will be deemed ineligible and will not be fulfilled. The exact prize value of each Instant Win ticket will be determined by comparing returned tickets with a prize value distribution list that has been preselected at random by computer. Prizes are valued in U.S. currency. For each one million, or part thereof, tickets distributed, the following prizes will be made available: 1 at $2,500 cash; 1 at $1,000 cash; 3 at $250 cash each; 5 at $50 cash each; 10 at $25 cash each; 1,000 at $1 cash each; and the balance at 50¢ cash each. Unclaimed prizes will not be awarded.

3. Winner claims are subject to verification by D. L. Blair, Inc., an independent judging organization whose decisions on all matters relating to this sweepstakes are final. Any returned tickets that are mutilated, tampered with, illegible or contain printing or other errors will be deemed automatically void. No responsibility is assumed for lost, late, nondelivered or misdirected mail. Taxes are the sole responsibility of winners. Limit: One (1) prize to a family, household or organization.

4. Offer open only to residents of the U.S. and Canada, 18 years of age or older, except employees of Harlequin Enterprises Limited, D. L. Blair, Inc., their agents and members of their immediate families. All federal, state, provincial, municipal and local laws apply. Offer void in Puerto Rico, the province of Quebec and wherever prohibited by law. All winners will receive their prize by mail. Taxes and/or duties are the sole responsibility of the winners. No substitution for prizes permitted. Major prize winners may be asked to sign and return an Affidavit of Eligibility within 30 days of notification. Noncompliance within this time or return of affidavit as undeliverable may result in disqualification, and prize may never be awarded. By acceptance of a prize, winners consent to the use of their names, photographs or other likeness for purposes of advertising, trade and promotion on behalf of Harlequin Enterprises Limited, without further compensation, unless prohibited by law. In order to win a prize, residents of Canada will be required to correctly answer a time-limited arithmetical skill-testing question to be administered by mail.

5. For a list of major prize winners (available after 2/14/97), send a self-addressed, stamped envelope to: "Instant Win 4229 Sweepstakes" Major Prize Winners, P.O. Box 4200, Blair, NE 68009-4200, U.S.A.

MILLION DOLLAR SWEEPSTAKES
OFFICIAL RULES
NO PURCHASE NECESSARY TO ENTER

1. To enter, follow the directions published. Method of entry may vary. For eligibility, entries must be received no later than March 31, 1998. No liability is assumed for printing errors, lost, late, non-delivered or misdirected entries.

   To determine winners, the sweepstakes numbers assigned to submitted entries will be compared against a list of randomly, preselected prize winning numbers. In the event all prizes are not claimed via the return of prize winning numbers, random drawings will be held from among all other entries received to award unclaimed prizes.

2. Prize winners will be determined no later than June 30, 1998. Selection of winning numbers and random drawings are under the supervision of D. L. Blair, Inc., an independent judging organization whose decisions are final. Limit: one prize to a family or organization. No substitution will be made for any prize, except as offered. Taxes and duties on all prizes are the sole responsibility of winners. Winners will be notified by mail. Odds of winning are determined by the number of eligible entries distributed and received.

3. Sweepstakes open to residents of the U.S. (except Puerto Rico), Canada and Europe who are 18 years of age or older, except employees and immediate family members of Torstar Corp., D. L. Blair, Inc., their affiliates, subsidiaries, and all other agencies, entities, and persons connected with the use, marketing or conduct of this sweepstakes. All applicable laws and regulations apply. Sweepstakes offer void wherever prohibited by law. Any litigation within the province of Quebec respecting the conduct and awarding of a prize in this sweepstakes must be submitted to the Régie des alcools, des courses et des jeux. In order to win a prize, residents of Canada will be required to correctly answer a time-limited arithmetical skill-testing question to be administered by mail.

4. Winners of major prizes (Grand through Fourth) will be obligated to sign and return an Affidavit of Eligibility and Release of Liability within 30 days of notification. In the event of non-compliance within this time period or if a prize is returned as undeliverable, D. L. Blair, Inc. may at its sole discretion, award that prize to an alternate winner. By acceptance of their prize, winners consent to use of their names, photographs or other likeness for purposes of advertising, trade and promotion on behalf of Torstar Corp., its affiliates and subsidiaries, without further compensation unless prohibited by law. Torstar Corp. and D. L. Blair, Inc., their affiliates and subsidiaries are not responsible for errors in printing of sweepstakes and prize winning numbers. In the event a duplication of a prize winning number occurs, a random drawing will be held from among all entries received with that prize winning number to award that prize.

5. This sweepstakes is presented by Torstar Corp., its subsidiaries and affiliates in conjunction with book, merchandise and/or product offerings. The number of prizes to be awarded and their value are as follows: Grand Prize — $1,000,000 (payable at $33,333.33 a year for 30 years); First Prize — $50,000; Second Prize — $10,000; Third Prize — $5,000; 3 Fourth Prizes — $1,000 each; 10 Fifth Prizes — $250 each; 1,000 Sixth Prizes — $10 each. Values of all prizes are in U.S. currency. Prizes in each level will be presented in different creative executions, including various currencies, vehicles, merchandise and travel. Any presentation of a prize level in a currency other than U.S. currency represents an approximate equivalent to the U.S. currency prize for that level, at that time. Prize winners will have the opportunity of selecting any prize offered for that level; however, the actual non U.S. currency equivalent prize if offered and selected, shall be awarded at the exchange rate existing at 3:00 P.M. New York time on March 31, 1998. A travel prize option, if offered and selected by winner, must be completed within 12 months of selection and is subject to: traveling companion(s) completing and returning of a Release of Liability prior to travel; and hotel and flight accommodations availability. For a current list of all prize options offered within prize levels, send a self-addressed, stamped envelope (WA residents need not affix postage) to: MILLION DOLLAR SWEEPSTAKES Prize Options, P.O. Box 4456, Blair, NE 68009-4456, USA.

6. For a list of prize winners (available after July 31, 1998) send a separate, stamped, self-addressed envelope to: MILLION DOLLAR SWEEPSTAKES Winners, P.O. Box 4459, Blair, NE 68009-4459, USA.

EXTRA BONUS PRIZE DRAWING
NO PURCHASE OR OBLIGATION NECESSARY TO ENTER

7. The Extra Bonus Prize will be awarded in a random drawing to be conducted no later than 5/30/98 from among all entries received. To qualify, entries must be received by 3/31/98 and comply with published directions. Prize ($50,000) is valued in U.S. currency. Prize will be presented in different creative expressions, including various currencies, vehicles, merchandise and travel. Any presentation in a currency other than U.S. currency represents an approximate equivalent to the U.S. currency value at that time. Prize winner will have the opportunity of selecting any prize offered in any presentation of the Extra Bonus Prize Drawing; however, the actual non U.S. currency equivalent prize, if offered and selected by winner, shall be awarded at the exchange rate existing at 3:00 P.M. New York time on March 31, 1998. For a current list of prize options offered, send a self-addressed, stamped envelope (WA residents need not affix postage) to: Extra Bonus Prize Options, P.O. Box 4462, Blair, NE 68009-4462, USA. All eligibility requirements and restrictions of the MILLION DOLLAR SWEEPSTAKES apply. Odds of winning are dependent upon number of eligible entries received. No substitution for prize except as offered. For the name of winner (available after 7/31/98), send a self-addressed, stamped envelope to: Extra Bonus Prize Winner, P.O. Box 4463, Blair, NE 68009-4463, USA.

SWP-H12CF1

Authors you'll treasure, books you'll want to keep!

Harlequin Romance books just keep getting better and better...and we're delighted to welcome you to our Simply the Best showcase for 1997.

Each month for a whole year we'll be highlighting a particular author—one we know you're going to love!

The year gets off to a great start with:

#3439 MARRIAGE BAIT
by Eva Rutland

Sparks fly when Lisa decides she isn't interested in a career—she wants a husband! Preferably a rich, glamorous one...and she'll do anything to catch one!

Available in January wherever Harlequin books are sold.

Free Gift Offer

With a Free Gift proof-of-purchase
from any Harlequin® book, you can receive
a beautiful cubic zirconia pendant.

This stunning marquise-shaped stone is a genuine cubic
zirconia—accented by an 18" gold tone necklace.
(Approximate retail value $19.95)

Send for yours today...
compliments of ✦HARLEQUIN®

To receive your free gift, a cubic zirconia pendant, send us one original proof-of-
purchase, photocopies not accepted, from the back of any Harlequin Romance®,
Harlequin Presents®, Harlequin Temptation®, Harlequin Superromance®, Harlequin
Intrigue®, Harlequin American Romance®, or Harlequin Historicals® title available in
August, September or October at your favorite retail outlet, together with the Free Gift
Certificate, plus a check or money order for $1.65 U.S./$2.15 CAN. (do not send cash) to
cover postage and handling, payable to Harlequin Free Gift Offer. We will send you the
specified gift. Allow 6 to 8 weeks for delivery. Offer good until December 31, 1996, or
while quantities last. Offer valid in the U.S. and Canada only.

Free Gift Certificate

Name: _____

Address: _____

City: _____ State/Province: _____ Zip/Postal Code: _____

Mail this certificate, one proof-of-purchase and a check or money order for postage
and handling to: HARLEQUIN FREE GIFT OFFER 1996. In the U.S.: 3010 Walden
Avenue, P.O. Box 9071, Buffalo NY 14269-9057. In Canada: P.O. Box 604, Fort Erie,
Ontario L2Z 5X3.

FREE GIFT OFFER   084-KMFR

ONE PROOF-OF-PURCHASE

To collect your fabulous FREE GIFT, a cubic zirconia pendant, you must include this
original proof-of-purchase for each gift with the properly completed Free Gift Certificate.

084-KMFR

Harlequin Romance ®

BABY BOOM

We are proud to announce the birth of our
new bouncing baby series—Baby Boom!

Each month in 1997 we'll be bringing you your very
own bundle of joy—a cute, delightful romance by one
of your favorite authors. Our heroes and heroines are
about to discover that two's company and three (or
four...or five) is a family!

This exciting new series is all about the true labor
of love...

Parenthood, and how to survive it!

Watch for:

#3442 TWO-PARENT FAMILY
by Patricia Knoll

Available in January wherever
Harlequin books are sold.

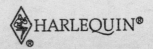